COLOR MY WORLD

A BAREFOOT BAY NOVELLA

MORGAN MALONE

FROM ROXANNE ST. CLAIRE

Dear Reader,

Welcome to Barefoot Bay World, a place for authors to write their own stories set in the tropical paradise that I created! For these books, I have only provided the setting of Mimosa Key and a cast of characters from my popular Barefoot Bay series. That's it! I haven't contributed to the plotting, writing, or editing of **Color My World**. This book is entirely the work of Morgan Malone, a popular author who has become a fan favorite in Barefoot Bay.

Not only do we have a lovely Holiday story, we get to revisit Missy Edmonds, a favorite secondary character from Morgan's first book in Barefoot Bay! This time, Missy's "friends with benefits" relationship with a Mimosa Key art gallery owner is starting to heat up. Is it just the mistletoe that's making their kisses more magical? Are those sparks from Hanukkah lights...or the real thing? Once again, this skilled author gives us a silver fox hero who can **Color My World** anytime!

Roxanne St. Claire

New York Times and *USA Today* bestselling author of the Barefoot Bay Series

www.roxannestclaire.com.

AUTHOR CREDITS

Color My World
    Edited and interior format by Deelylah Mullin
    Cover Art by Kris Norris
    Published by Morgan Malone
    Digital Release: September 2018

This story is set in a world created by Roxanne St. Claire as the Barefoot Bay series, and this work has been published with her permission. Information and links to Roxanne St. Claire's Barefoot Bay books can be found at http://www.roxannestclaire.com/barefoot-bay-series.

To Missy: my housekeeper, assistant, dog sitter and friend. I couldn't function without you.

To Rich and Mike: two artists for whom I have the utmost respect and affection.

To Lorraine: you taught me how to paint again.

And for MLH. Always.

CHAPTER ONE

It was an almost perfect start to the day. Gamboge, tangerine, and violet streaked across a cerulean sky, scents of salt and sea wafted on a gentle breeze, and in his hands, the welcoming weight of a stoneware mug filled to the brim with hot, dark coffee. And ten pounds of orange fur draped across his bare feet. Meowing plaintively. He was unmoved.

Don gazed down at the large marmalade cat. She stared right back at him, her imperious green eyes demanding action. He took a long sip of coffee.

The cat rose, turned away, and flicked her tail as she strolled across the cottage's living room toward the bedroom. When she was only two steps to the bedroom door, Don moved quickly away from the front window, reaching the kitchen in only five steps. The cat paused. When she heard the refrigerator door open, she looked at the scowling man. Her eyes brightened and she pranced back to his side. When he bent to pour the remainder of the carton of cream into the bowl at his feet, she twined herself once around his ankles then settled to lapping it up.

"Lady, you are such a conniving little bitch."

The cat looked up disdainfully, as if the epithet meant nothing to her, and returned to her breakfast.

"But, you control us with a great deal of panache, I'll give you that." Don's long, lean fingers tipped the mug slightly in the cat's direction, as if offering a toast. Putting up with a persnickety cat was a small price to pay for the privilege of being Missy Edmond's sometimes lover. Or, as she liked to say, in her husky, Lauren Bacall voice, "friend with benefits".

Glancing down the hall to the bedroom door, Don considered delaying his departure for his studio. Not a good idea. Now that Missy did not have to be up at the crack of dawn to ensure that Dr. Levi Gould had his breakfast, briefcase, and details of the day, she had been loving sleeping in till eight in the morning. And it had been well after midnight when they had finally untangled themselves and curled up to sleep, with the requisite foot of space between them. Missy was no cuddler—and for that, Don was grateful.

He finished his coffee in three quick gulps, washed his mug and left it on the drain board. Tossing the empty cream container into the trash, he looked around to see if Missy's demanding feline, aptly named Lady Marmalade—both for the color of her fur and her regal attitude—was lurking about. He spied her on the fluffy indigo cushion of the white wicker rocker placed at just the right angle to catch the first rays of morning sun through the room's large east-facing window, lazily licking at her orange and white paws. Satisfied that that both the females in the cottage would be settled for at least another hour, Don eased his feet into his scuffed deck shoes and slipped out the front door.

He loved the early mornings on Mimosa Key, especially here, at Levi's spreading acreage on the northern coast of the island. The light was so clear, the colors so intense—gazing toward the beach through the foliage that surrounded the yard was like taking inventory of his artist's palette. He imagined a large landscape, in oils, that might capture the play of the sunlight on the gently lapping waves, like diamonds strewn across a swath of turquoise silk. The slamming of a door roused him from his reverie. Levi strode over the broad front porch of his house, just across the wide circular drive from Missy's cottage, briefcase in one hand and travel mug in the other. The surgeon was nattily dressed as always, from crisply knotted silk tie to perfectly polished black loafers, his salt and pepper hair—neatly combed—still damp from the shower.

Ruefully glancing down at his faded grey sweatshirt—torn cuff shoved up his right arm—and his ancient khakis with a splotch of blue paint near his left knee, Don moved silently over to his dusty black Jeep and slid behind the wheel. He loved the Doc, like a brother, but he was damned if he could put up with his annoying cheeriness at five after seven in the morning. Especially today. Better to just sit quietly in the Jeep until Levi rounded the corner of his house to the car port where Don knew he'd left his Mercedes parked the night before. Levi would never notice him.

He needn't have worried. The Doc's bride of four months was jogging down the drive to the house, her bright pink running gear like a flash of flamingo in the sunlight. Spying her husband, Ella broke into a dash, reaching Levi in seconds. Throwing herself into his arms, heedless of briefcase and travel mug, she planted a kiss on him that was so loud Don could hear it twenty feet away. And he felt a little piece of his heart break. Again.

Oblivious to him, and to their chocolate Lab, Hersch, who was dancing around them, the couple remained locked in a tight embrace. Don started up the Jeep and pulled away from Missy's cottage, heading down the driveway and out to the beach road.

The cool morning breeze should have cleared his mind but memories from his troubled past crowded in. December 1, 2005. Thirteen years' worth of pain and sorrow had been brought front and center by the sight of Ella and Levi wrapped in each other's arms. He did not begrudge his friend his late-in-life happiness. Don was grateful he had Missy—a warm and willing woman with whom he passed many evenings and some mornings laughing and loving. But some days, and many nights, he cursed God, the Fates, the universe, and the twisty, turning mountainous roads that had destroyed his own bliss.

As he pulled up to the light at the Four Way, Don realized he was muttering in Italian. *Dannazione.* It was not often he slipped into his native language, but, if there was any day of the year that would pull him back into his past, it was the first day of December. He decided to forego a second cup of coffee, if you could call it that, from the Super Min and made a right at the light. Within minutes, he was pulling up to the rear of his business. It had become his home, this awkward white building with faded blue trim and a crushed seashell parking lot in the back. He strode purposefully up the short flight of stairs to the blue door and punched in his security code. The interior was cool as he entered the storage area that took up the space in the back. Passing down a short hallway to the front of his store, he did not flip on any lights. It was too early to open the gallery and framing shop that occupied most of the main floor. Instead, he took the steps of the ancient wooden stairway two at a time to the upper level. This, truly, was his home.

The second floor was what had become popularly known as open-concept. Don snorted at the notion that one huge room could now be the most-sought after design feature on all the HGTV shows Missy watched constantly. He had always preferred defined spaces, but he had neither the time nor the inclination to divide up his living space. There was no way he was going to hide the magnificent view of the Gulf revealed by the three huge windows making up the front wall. It was there, looking out at the water, he had located his studio.

He'd arranged a low table with a sofa and two chairs to break the space between his painting area and the kitchen located in the center of the main room. Behind the kitchen was a large bathroom. His sleeping space was at the back. Don had intended to grab a quick shower before he opened the shop but the early morning image of the sun on the waves outside Missy's cottage called to him. He switched on his sound system and threw a three-by-four-foot canvas up on the easel. As the strains of *La Traviata* flowed around him, his hands mixed the blues he envisioned for the painting. Already lost in the seascape, the sad memories of the day faded from his mind.

CHAPTER TWO

Her fingers crept along the cool smoothness of the linen sheets, searching for the warmth of her lover. It was not until her arm was stretched almost straight that she encountered a mass of body heat. Covered with fur.

"Well, hell." Missy's throaty voice echoed in the high ceiling of her bedroom. "Lady, looks like it's you and me." The cat rolled over on her side, her paws playfully batting at Missy's fingers, her purring competing with the soft moans of her owner, as Missy stretched and yawned into complete wakefulness. The two females, human and feline, enjoyed another few moments of languor until Missy's eyes strayed to the alarm clock on the nightstand.

"Damn it! It's almost eight o'clock!" Missy jumped out of bed and dashed into the adjoining bathroom. Within ten minutes she had quickly washed up, brushing her teeth in the shower, and had twisted her long, dark hair into a messy up do. Five more minutes had her clad in a simple white, long-sleeved T-shirt and faded jeans. She emptied expensive salmon cat food into Lady's bowl while she shimmied her feet into the moccasins she had kicked off near the kitchen the night before. "Well," she muttered to the meowing cat, "truth be told, they fell off when Don picked me up and carried me to the bedroom last night. But, who's complaining, right?" The events of the night before made her cheeks heat up. She still felt a thrill when Don lifted her effortlessly into his arms. He was not a big guy, but he was in such great shape that every inch of him was like steel. Every. Damn. Inch. Her blush grew hotter.

A few quick pets while the cat daintily devoured her breakfast, and Missy was out the door. She paused to do a quick 360-degree turn, surveying the property with a practiced eye. Several palm fronds were down along the edge of the lawn. The white crushed shells that covered the drive were uneven in a few spots. Planters on either side of the front steps to the main house needed refreshing and her own window boxes were looking downright pathetic. Stashing her observations away in the organized file cabinet that was her mind, Missy's long legs quickly brought her to the broad porch of Levi's—and now, Ella's—house. The thought of her former bad-boy bachelor boss now settled into marital bliss brought a broad smile to Missy's face as she unlocked the front door.

Hersch greeted her as soon as she entered the foyer. "Hey, Hersch! How you doin', boy? Did you miss me since, oh, seven o'clock last night?" Missy ruffled the fur on the thick neck of the chocolate Lab and planted a kiss on his large head, before ambling into the kitchen. The coffee maker needed refilling before she took a cup coffee, but as she set another pot to brew, the strong aroma made her slightly queasy. "I am *not* getting sick," she thought, "I have way too much to do this week."

Opting for tea instead, Missy popped a mug of hot water into the microwave. Before she had a chance to toss the lemon ginger herbal tea bag into the trash, Ella wandered into the kitchen. Her hair stood up in damp blonde spikes, a loose long-sleeved T-shirt topped pink flowered leggings and feet tucked into fuzzy slippers—evidence that the author was readying herself for a full day of work on her latest book.

"I smell fresh coffee. I am in desperate need. Thank you, girl-friend!" Unscrewing the cap of her insulated mug, Ella splashed coffee on the counter in her haste to fill her cup. "Did you know I was such a klutz when you met me, Missy? It's a wonder I can get dressed in the morning." Ella turned, laughing, to lean against the counter and smile at Missy.

The two women had become fast friends and allies, joined by their love of Dr. Levi Gould and their genuine affection for each other. Missy had been taking care of Doc, as she usually called him, since she had arrived on Mimosa Key three years earlier. Though Levi had been known by the nickname Dr. Hottie Rock Star because of his drop-dead gorgeousness and his skill as an orthopedic surgeon, Missy had almost immediately christened him Dr. Stray Dog Magnet. Levi had already adopted Hersch, an abandoned dog left by owners who had fled the hurricane that had eventually led to the rebirth of Mimosa Key. Within twenty-four hours of meeting Missy in his walk-in orthopedic clinic, Levi had hired her to be caretaker at the property he'd recently purchased along the north coast of the island. She had lived for months in the little cottage she still occupied while the main house—virtually destroyed by the hurricane—was rebuilt to Levi's exacting standards. Levi had stayed at one of the villas at Casa Blanca Resort and Spa and put in long hours building up the FL-Ortho practice, while Missy supervised the teams of workers restoring the old house and extensive property. She had become the glue that held the busy surgeon's life together: house-keeper, cook, property manager, dog-sitter, and administrative assistant. Until the Doc met Ella, Missy had been the one constant female presence in his life. And he had been the only man she trusted completely.

"Ella, I thank God every day that you are a brilliant author and terrific wife, but especially that you are a klutz who cannot cook, do laundry, water plants, or hammer a nail into a wall. It gives me job security. That you run with Hersch every morning is your one saving grace." Missy smirked as she sipped her herbal tea. "And that you love Levi and have put light in his eyes, at last."

The tall slender blonde laughed at Missy's words. "It's true. I was never taught basic *womanly* skills when I was a kid. I did learn, however, how to wheedle special treats from the cook or get the housekeeper to hem my skirts a little shorter than my mom would have liked. When you are the child of a doctor and a lawyer, them's the breaks, I guess. But, I managed to survive for thirty years or so on my own...and take-out menus, laundries that pick up and deliver, and kind-hearted maintenance guys. If you can't do anything but your job, New York City is the place to live."

Missy's face froze as she listened to Ella's assessment of her upbringing as the privileged daughter of high-powered professionals. She gulped when she realized Ella had stopped laughing and was staring at her. Ella had been a criminal prosecutor for years before she became a best-selling author and her eyes had narrowed with investigative gleam.

"What's wrong, Missy? Did I say something to upset you?" Ella pointed to the stools that lined the kitchen island. "Come here and sit for a minute. You look positively green."

"It's nothing, Ella. I'm a bit queasy this morning. Either the scallops I made for dinner last night aren't sitting right in my stomach or I'm coming down with the stomach crud that everyone seemed to be getting last week." But, Missy gratefully eased down onto a seat next to Ella.

"I call bullshit on that, Missy. The scallops last night were delicious. And while you may be falling victim to the stomach virus that's been making the rounds, that would not account for the bleak unhappiness I can see in your eyes. So, spill the beans, girlfriend. What did I say that upset you so much? And I'm sorry for that. You know how much we love you. Levi and I, and Hersch." Ella patted her dog's head before laying her hand on Missy's clammy palm.

Missy was about to say, "It's nothing, you've been writing crime novels for too long—you're suspicious of everything." The words were on her lips. But what came out instead, in a torrent of emotion that few on the island had ever seen, was "That was my life you just described. That was me."

CHAPTER THREE

E lla took a long sip of coffee and said, simply, "Tell me."

Missy wrapped her chilled hands around her mug of tea, staring for a long moment into its golden depths. Taking a deep breath, she looked up at Ella, and began.

"Levi knows some of my story. I could not, in good conscience, come to work for him, move into the cottage and later, freely wander in and out of this house—his home—without telling him about me." Missy laughed bitterly. "The man is such a softie. I could have been an axe-murderer for all he knew. He looked at my beat-up shoulder and thought he knew everything about me. He was sure I was an abused wife or girlfriend, on the run. And he gave me shelter. That's when I knew he was Dr. Stray Dog Magnet, not Hottie Rock Star. Although he *is* pretty hot."

Nodding at the near perfect-description of her husband, Ella patted Missy's hand. She motioned her hand in a "go on" gesture, encouraging her friend to continue.

"So, he was wrong about me. I wasn't an abused wife. But, I was running away. From my life." Missy took a sip of tea and glanced out the window at the still green vista, the bright blue sky. "I can't get used to not seeing snow on December first. I still miss the snow." She turned back to Ella. "I grew up in Boston. Back Bay Boston. My parents were successful importers, very committed to their careers. And to each other. My mother got pregnant at 45. She thought I was the onset of menopause. But, I was, as she later told me, an unfortunate accident. I think she considered an abortion but my father was Catholic and against it. And, as it turned out, she was almost five months pregnant when she discovered her upset stomach and fatigue was me and not chronic indigestion."

A disdainful snort from Ella had Missy ruefully smiling. "Yeah, I know. What kind of mother tells her daughter that she was a mistake? My mother, that's who. She got through the pregnancy easily and I was born without much fuss. I think she was back in the office within three weeks. And I was in the hands of a nurse, then a nanny, then the housekeeper and cook. I was in pre-school and after-school programs from the time I entered kindergarten. Someone on staff dropped me off and picked me up. The housekeeper supervised my homework and the cook gave me breakfast and dinner. Sometimes, two or three days would go by when I did not see my parents."

Missy paused. Ella's face was unreadable but her fingers were tightly wrapped around her coffee mug, knuckles white against her pale golden skin.

"Don't get me wrong. It was no great loss. Many kids I knew were in similar situations. Busy parents, with lots of money, who could hire people to do everything parents are supposed to do. Except be parents. But, I was not unhappy. I liked being alone with my books, my dolls, and my stuffed animals. I read to them, made them tea parties. I took piano lessons for years and I would set up all my 'babies' on the settee in the music room and perform for them." But she had been lonely—and the loneliness of those years swept over Missy as she related her story to Ella. Shaking off the cold fingers of the past, she continued.

"I graduated from prep school and went off to college. Smith—my mother's alma mater. I wanted to major in education; I wanted to teach little kids. But, my parents pushed me toward something with *more of a future*, as they described it. I got a double degree in government and economics, spent a year in Paris. My parents were from France, so they were pleased that I was being exposed to my heritage. Though there was not much of my mother's family left after the Nazis. My mother was Jewish." Ella's gasp of astonishment stopped Missy's reverie.

"You're Jewish? Does Levi know?" Ella was shaking her head. "My god, Missy, that's a lot of information for me to process first thing in the morning."

"Yeah, I told him. He was amazed I could make brisket. So, I told him I was Jewish. What I didn't tell him was that I learned how to make it by watching Food Network on my laptop. Like I learned how to cook or bake everything. Almost everything I do around here, I learned by watching television or by Googling it."

"You're amazing, Missy. I can't believe you run this house and this property and do all that you do. All I can do is write."

"Yeah. I can write, too. Though not like you." Missy's laugh was hollow. "After college, I went to DC. I got a job in a political consulting firm. You know that show 'Scandal'?" That was me. We represented mostly politicians. I wrote position statements, news releases—just about everything. Then, I got involved in organizing campaigns. I'm great with details and what I don't know, I know how to find out. I did well; I was kick-ass good. I had a townhouse in Georgetown, more money than I could ever spend, and fabulous shoes!" Looking down at her beat-up moccasins, Missy shook her head in wonder at what her life had been. "But, I wasn't happy. I just worked and worked. I wanted to be the best, I guess, to make my parents finally notice me. But, they never did. I was still an unnecessary amendment to their lives. They died four years ago. My father went first—a stroke took him early one morning as he was reading the papers. Within three months, my mother suffered a massive heart attack in her sleep. The housekeeper found her."

"Oh, Missy, I'm so sorry. I can't imagine losing both parents so close to each other. How dreadful for you!" Ella gave her a fierce hug.

"Thank you, but you know, it was better they went almost together. They were each other's whole lives—no one else mattered. And it was as if I was superfluous again. All the arrangements had been made—funeral, cremation, sale of the house and everything in it, distribution of their assets to various endowments and charities. And a trust for me. Quarterly stipends until I reach forty. Almost thirty-five years of my life disposed of within weeks. It was numbing. Oddly, I missed them. I came to the realization I had no one in the world who was connected to me in any personal way, whatsoever."

Getting up from the stool, Missy stretched then moved over to place her mug in the sink. Leaning back against the counter she faced Ella, rubbing both her arms as if she were freezing. But she was trying to find the words to finish her narrative—to tie her former life up into neat details.

"And that's when things got really interesting. I guess, because I was lonely, I finally accepted one of the offers that frequently came my way in Washington. Powerful men look for women with power and/or money. I had both. He was handsome, intelligent, and an influential lobbyist. I let him seduce me. It was a whirlwind at first, very heady. Then, I began to think we might actually have some kind of future. Until I came home late one night and found him in bed with another woman—some senator's administrative assistant. I ran out of the house so fast, I missed the last three steps. That's how I wrenched my shoulder. But, I rented a car and drove south. I'd heard about Casa Blanca Resort and Spa from a woman at work who'd come here for a wedding. That's why I came to Mimosa Key. And it was good strategy because I figured everyone would be expecting me to go back to Boston. By the time I arrived here, my arm was really hurting. So, I ended up in Levi's clinic. He 'adopted' me and offered me a place to live with interesting work to do. I'd thought to hide out at the resort—not the best idea, maybe. But no one would look for me working as a caretaker and living in a tiny cottage. Oddly, I became a damn good housekeeper, cook, dog sitter, and handywoman. And I love it. I love my cottage, I love this property, and I love Hersch and Lady. And you guys. You and Doc are my family. My first *real* family."

Missy walked back to where Ella sat with her eyes wide in astonishment, Ella's low wolf whistle—of admiration?—was loud in the silence of the kitchen. Missy held out her hand to Ella and said, "Since I've just spilled my guts to you, I should probably introduce myself. I'm Melisande Emond. Nice to meet you."

CHAPTER FOUR

The light coming through the windows was too bright. Don looked up from the painting. Outside, the sun was almost directly overhead. He glanced over at the clock on the microwave oven. "Jesus. It's almost noon!"

Wiping his hands on a rag hanging from the side of his easel, he stepped back to survey his morning's work. He'd captured the deep indigo blue of the sky just beginning to lighten from the rising sun. The middle of the seascape was still blank, to leave room for the colors of the sunrise. Shades of ultramarine blue and turquoise made up the bottom of the painting, the darkness of the sea waiting for the sun to cast diamonds of light upon its surface. Don felt the muscles in his face stretch in a satisfied grin, remembering the words of one of his favorite instructors at art school. "It's a good start."

The sound of fists pounding on the front door of his shop forced him to turn away from the canvas and hurry down the creaking staircase to the first floor. He could see Clay Walker peering through the glass insert in the front door. "*Calmati, calmati.* Calm down," he was muttering as he opened the door to one of the few people he liked *and* trusted on Mimosa Key.

"Were you sleeping or painting? I've been hammering on this door for ages!" Clay pushed past him into the dim shadows of the gallery. "You haven't even turned the lights on in here! What's the deal—too late a night or too early a morning?"

Shaking his head and smiling, Don closed the door and stepped into the gallery, flipping on lights as he moved into the large space. The walls were covered with scenes from Mimosa Key and the Florida coast, all painted in oils by Don in the years since he moved to the small island community. Early on, it was his framing business that produced the most income. But since the building of Casa Blanca Resort and Spa, designed by Clay and owned by his lovely wife, Lacey Armstrong, his oil paintings of the beautiful beach at Barefoot Bay had been his best sellers.

Clay stood in the middle of the gallery, hands on his hips, his eyes roaming the walls. "Man, I am in need of some paintings. Like, right now!"

"Well, you've come to the right place because if there's anything I've got, its paintings. Because, as you may have noticed, I'm an artist." Don was laughing as he threw his arm over the younger man's shoulder. "What has you so riled up today? Are you having an art emergency?"

"Laugh all you want, old man, but that is exactly what is going on. My wife, the lovely and talented Lacey, is in dire need of at least ten large seascapes for the villas at Casa Blanca." Clay's voice was not at all amused.

"What do you mean? Every one of the villas has at least one of my paintings in each bedroom and another in the living room. A few more in the large villas. Is she tired of them and looking for replacements? I thought she loved those paintings." Even as the resort was being built, Lacey had commissioned Don to produce oils that showcased Barefoot Bay and other Mimosa Key landmarks, like Pleasure Pointe Beach and Barefoot Mountain. His paintings hung in all the villas and several were prominently placed in Casa Blanca's main building and Junonia, the resort's restaurant.

"She loved every one of those paintings. But you know my wife, she's a canny businesswoman. We had a large family reunion booked through Thanksgiving. The mom and dad were the last to check out, just a couple days ago. The family had such a fantastic time at the resort that they've already booked five villas for next year. But, the parents decided the best Christmas gift they could give to their children was the artwork from the specific villa each of their children and grandchildren stayed in! So, almost every piece of art from Bay Laurel, Artemisia, Saffron, Acacia, and African Daisy were shipped out today. Lacey sold them all and she made a damn good profit, let me tell you." Clay pulled an envelope from his pocket and shoved it in Don's hands. "She was reluctant to sell them but the father just kept upping his offer until it was more than twice as much as we paid you for them. Lacey couldn't say no to that. Especially with the possibility of losing the reservation for five villas for next year if she didn't acquiesce. So, here's a check for half the profit from the sale. And we need replacement art pronto because all the villas are rented for most of December."

Don stared at the envelope and then at the agitated architect. And burst out laughing. "You just said too much, my friend. Now that I know how desperate you are, I could jack up the price on every painting in here. You are no business man. You should have sent Lacey!"

Clay just grinned at the amused artist. Don's reserve and reticence to talk money were almost as well known in Mimosa Key as his talent with a paint brush. Most of the time, he seemed almost reluctant to name a price for his work—especially if the customer was a local. Tourists paid the full price most of the time, unless Don took a liking to them or felt sorry for them or any of a dozen other reasons. Clay worried a bit about his friend, wondering how he managed to live on what must be an erratic income. But, looking at him, he knew the answer. Don was usually dressed in old chinos or jeans, often with a paint stain somewhere, and worn sweatshirts or T-shirts. He had one suit for weddings and funerals, lived in rooms above his shop, and drove an ancient Jeep. Clay had heard Don say more than once that his only luxuries were Russian sable brushes and imported San Marzano tomatoes for his famous spaghetti sauce.

"I'll be honest with you. I'd probably pay any price you name. Lacey's on a tear and I don't want her upset with the holidays approaching. But, I know you and you won't screw around with me on this—you love my wife too much." Clay turned back to count the framed paintings hung in the small gallery. "Buddy, I have to tell you, I'm just about going to clean you out here. I need all of these...and then some."

"These are just the paintings I've had time to mount and frame. Come upstairs and I'll show you the rest. I can have them framed and ready to go in a couple of days. The ones down here you can take with you today. That should put a smile on Lacey's face." Don headed out of the gallery and up the stairs. He turned and laughed at Clay. "That is until you get my bill." The younger man's groans followed Don up the stairs.

Walking into the studio, Clay's eyes immediately fell on the painting Don had begun that morning. He was literally pulled to the unfinished canvas and stood, studying it for several minutes. "That's the north shore. Levi's beach. I don't think we have any paintings like this. I must have this one. How soon can you finish it?"

Clay turned to the artist, determination evident in his expression.

Don schooled his face into an impassive mask, resolving to withstand any argument or offer his friend made. He shook his head. "That one is not for sale."

"C'mon, man. Lacey will love it. She might even want it for herself. You gotta let me have it."

"Nope. Not for sale." Don's voice was firm. He was not going to sell this painting and he was not exactly sure why. Staring at the brilliant blues he had spent the morning mixing and layering on the canvas, the answer suddenly came to him. The sky and the sea were the color of Missy's eyes. Deep, dark blue, with just a hint of green. "It's a gift for someone."

"Are you giving it to Levi and Ella? Damn, they already have a dozen of your paintings—not to mention Levi's infamous mural. Cut me a break—I know Lacey will love it. It will be the perfect Christmas present." Clay was used to getting his way.

"It's for Missy." The words were out of Don's mouth before he knew it. *Where had that thought come from?* Then he smiled to himself. Missy would love the painting. It would look perfect hanging above her white wicker bed.

"For Missy? Well, damn, I can't argue with that. She's a lucky woman. I am sorry I pushed you, but I didn't know you two were getting serious. I don't know what she sees in your scraggy ass but this painting will keep her too happy to notice what an old curmudgeon you are."

Startled, Don just stared at Clay for a moment. *Serious?* He wasn't serious about Missy. They were good friends, but that was all. Well, that and the mind-blowing sex—but that was it. *Wasn't it?*

Determined to avoid further speculation by Clay, Don quickly went over to the wall and began turning finished canvases toward his eager buyer. Within the next thirty minutes, Clay had selected another dozen paintings, including one that was destined for Lacey. By the time the two men had loaded the dozen framed paintings from the gallery into Clay's SUV and come to terms on their price and the amount that would be due when Don delivered the remaining art work in two days, the sun was dipping low in the sky. The studio and gallery were almost empty and Don's stomach was rumbling.

Back upstairs, he stared into a barren refrigerator and cursed himself for not stopping at the Super Min that morning. Now, he would have to drive over to the convenience store and deal with Charity Grambling's inevitable cross-examination or try to sneak in and out of South of the Border without being pulled into a conversation over one or two beers. He was not in the mood for socializing.

"Don, are you upstairs?" The melodic voice of Ella Anderson drifted up from the first floor.

Another interruption. Slightly annoyed, he moved toward the stairway to call down to her. "Yeah, I'll be right there."

"Don't bother. I have something for you. Can I come up?" He heard her footsteps on the creaky stairs. *Damn.* Plastering a pleasant smile on his face, he emerged from the studio just as Ella reached the top step.

Her spiky blonde hair was windblown and her cheeks were flushed. In her hands was a casserole dish wrapped in a bright blue dish towel. "Here." She thrust it into his hands. "It's hot and its heavy. Damn thing weighs a ton!"

The spicy aroma of sauce and cheese wafted up from the heavy stoneware as he carried it into the kitchen area and placed it on the stovetop. Ella was digging in the tote bag slung on her shoulder. "Missy made a ton of eggplant parmesan today and two loaves of garlic bread. When I said I was coming into town to speak to you, she insisted I bring this with me. She figured you'd be painting all day and since she wasn't going to see you tonight, she wanted to make sure you had something to eat."

The low rumble from Don's stomach had Ella laughing as she placed the foil-wrapped bread on the kitchen island. "I don't know how that woman always knows when someone needs to eat, but she's almost never wrong."

Don didn't know what to say. His mind was awash with conflicting emotions. He was grateful for the food but annoyed Missy felt she had to send him dinner—like he didn't know how to take care of himself. He wanted to be alone today, but he had enjoyed dickering with Clay over the price for his paintings. He guarded his privacy but it was nice that Ella, his best friend's wife, felt comfortable just walking into his space. He realized then that the barriers he had built around his life, around his heart, had been breached in many small ways by his few close friends on Mimosa Key.

"Well, thank you. And thank Missy too. I forgot she had that soap-making class tonight with Frankie. My refrigerator is empty, so you've saved me a trip to Charity's lair."

Ella grimaced at Charity's name. The woman loved Levi but merely tolerated Ella. "I'd settle for peanut butter on crackers before I'd voluntarily subject myself to another of her lectures about how lucky I am that Levi married me. I know she approved of our marriage but I still get the feeling she thinks I'm not quite good enough for him."

Ella glanced around the studio. "You've been busy today, Don. Looks like you have some framing to do and...is that a new painting on the easel? Oh, I love it! That's our beach, isn't it?" Like Clay, Ella was drawn to the unfinished oil. She stood, chin cupped in one hand, staring at the painting. "You had to know I would want this painting for Levi—and if he saw it, he would insist upon getting it for me. But, I'm not going to try to talk you into selling it to me because I know this view. It's from the front of Missy's cottage, isn't it? I'm thinking it's a Hanukkah present for her?"

Turning to the painter, Ella was grinning. "She will love it, you know. The blues are perfect, exactly what the Gulf looked like this morning. And the water is the same color as Missy's eyes."

"When I saw the beach view this morning outside the cottage, I knew I had to paint it. I spent all morning on it today. When I stepped back to look at it, I realized I had to give it to Missy. I'm sure I can finish it by Christmas, but what did you mean by Hanukkah present? Missy's not Jewish...is she?" Don could not remember ever discussing religion with his lover. Come to think of it, he couldn't remember discussing anything of importance with Missy—just daily activities, harmless gossip about the island's population. And amazing sex. They did it more than they talked about it. But they *did* talk about sex a lot.

"Yeah, she's Jewish. Her mom was Jewish and that makes her a member of the Tribe." Ella laughed again. "So, that cuts into your painting time since Hanukkah starts on December twelfth, this year. A gift like this is definitely a 'first night' gift, so that gives you less than two weeks."

Ella walked back to Don, fumbling in her shoulder bag again. She pulled a photograph out of its depths and handed it to him. He saw a picture of Ella, driving down Levi's driveway, in her red Mustang convertible, Hersch in the passenger seat, ears flying back and a big drooling grin on his doggie face. "This is the reason I came to see you today. I'm on the same deadline. I wanted to ask you to paint this picture into the mural in Levi's surgical suite. He doesn't have me or Hersch on his wall of toys and I think I rate at least as high as the ATV. I'm sure Hersch is as important as the Jaguar, or maybe a close second..." She broke off when Don started shaking his head, *no*.

"I don't do portraits. I can't paint this picture on Doc's wall." His answer was curt, his tone clearly indicating that for him, the subject was closed. He should have known that his firm reply would do no good. Ella had been a high-powered criminal prosecutor before she began her writing career and she was not going to take no for an answer. Ella pulled another photo from her bag. This one showed the rear of the car, heading down the white seashell driveway. The short blonde hair on the back of Ella's head caught the sunlight, her right hand was raised in a jaunty wave and only Hersch's head was visible over the headrest on the passenger seat.

"How about this one? No faces equal no portraits. C'mon, Don, you have got help me out. What else do I get for the man who has everything and who buys what he doesn't have faster than my Grammy at a flea market. Say yes now because I gonna harass you 'til you do, and you know I'll win. And I need it done before December twelfth. Pretty please!"

It took another half hour to get Ella to leave. Or, he thought with real admiration for her skills, another twenty-five minutes for Ella to wear him down and convince him to put her and her hot car into Levi's mural plus five minutes of her gloating, even after he named his price. Now, it was getting on to twilight, the sky was darkening and so was Don's mood. He shoved Clay's envelope and Ella's check into a drawer in the kitchen island that served as his deposit box. When he saw the number of checks and the roll of bills crammed into the drawer, he swore softly. "*Madre de Dio.* I need to get to the bank in Miami soon. Maybe tomorrow morning. Early. And I'll get some more supplies while I'm out. And groceries," he thought, as his stomach growled again.

He dished up some of the eggplant parmesan and let it cool while he poured himself a large glass of red wine. Turning on one light in the studio, he walked to the closet built into the wall just off the entryway. Don set his wine glass on the floor and fumbled with the lock. When the door swung open, he sank to his knees. Through the tears that were already flowing, he stared at the reasons he no longer painted portraits. From canvases and sheets of watercolor paper, the beautiful face of his wife, Gina, and his little son, his *bambino*, Raphael, stared back at him. *Miei cari, miei cari*...my darlings.

CHAPTER FIVE

"**D**amn. I make great garlic bread!" Missy sucked melted butter off her finger tips and reached for her glass of red wine. Lady Marmalade was sitting in the wicker chair next to her. The cat's deep green eyes darted from Missy's fingers to the near-empty plate on the small table between them. A tiny piece of bread remained and all that was left of the eggplant parmesan was a smear of red sauce, with a sprinkling of parmesan cheese.

"You know I love you and you've been very polite, so here you go." As soon as Missy put the blue stoneware plate down on the ground, the cat leapt gracefully from her perch. A thorough licking was accompanied by a satisfied purr. Missy leaned back in her chair to enjoy the view of cat, garden and sea.

Her little patio off the cottage's kitchen had just enough room for two chairs and the small pedestal table. A compact but efficient grill sat off to the side and that was it. But it was more than enough for Missy. Herbs and flowers filled the bright blue planters surrounding the patio, except for the walkway to the beach. White crushed seashells gleamed pearl-like in the waning sunlight, the path meandering between lush foliage and manicured lawn. Located on the side of the cottage away from the main house, this was Missy's private oasis.

Levi had offered to expand the cottage since Missy had moved in, but she had refused. As the owner, of course, Levi could do what he wanted with the property but he had generally acquiesced to Missy's pleas to keep the cottage simple and small. "I have to clean your damn mini-mansion every day, Doc," she often reminded him. "I don't want to come home and have to do the same damn thing in my place." The good doctor had been as understanding as his natural builder's soul would allow. He had contented himself with ordering a new roof, new windows, new siding, a new bathroom, and a modern kitchen for the little cottage. If a few walls got moved during the upgrades, well, it made the Doc happy. And Missy did not begrudge him because she loved the cottage and was eternally grateful to Levi for giving her a home.

"It doesn't get much better than this, Lady." Missy sighed the words as her cat leapt up onto her lap and curled, purring, into a mass of orange and white fluff. Levi might have found the bedraggled kitten near his office several months earlier, but the cat had become Missy's constant companion almost from the first. A fact which warmed Missy's heart and satisfied Hersch, still the top dog on the estate.

"I never had a pet before you, Lady. No animals allowed in that pristine Back Bay mansion or in that stylized Georgetown brownstone. Nope, my girl, you and I are both unwanted orphans. I guess that makes us family." A feline headbutt to Missy's hand was evidence of Lady's agreement.

They sat quietly in the dusky light, listening to the sound of the waves breaking on Levi's dock. Missy sipped the dark red Barolo, enjoying its rich silkiness. It was the last of a case Don had brought over during the summer. The man liked his Italian reds, that was for sure. Her mind catalogued her lover's tastes in wine—Italian, always —and food, steak or pasta and any kind of shellfish. He loved anything chocolate for dessert but he had a weakness for tiramisu. As her mind drifted, it occurred to her that he seemed to favor Italian cuisine, alcohol, and sweets.

Hmm, maybe he comes from an Italian family? With a last name like Smith, he could be anything. In a nation of immigrants, she knew that many sojourners from foreign shores had ended up with new generic last names when they came through Ellis Island in the late 1800s through mid-1900s. Her own French-born parents had been immigrants after World War II but they had been allowed to keep their French surnames.

The air was turning chilly, so Missy scooped up her sleeping cat and her dirty dishes and ambled into the cozy warmth of the cottage. After depositing Lady on her favorite chair and the dishes in the dishwasher, she made short work of cleaning up the kitchen. Yawning, she glanced at the microwave and realized that it was almost nine o'clock. And she hadn't heard from Don. They had made no plans for the evening—they rarely did on the days she had soap-making class at Francesca's goat farm—but there was almost always a daily text from him. Sometimes just checking in, sometimes with a chatty message— usually gossip he had picked up at the Super Min from Charity's acerbic tongue. But, more and more frequently of late, it was an inquiry about spending some time together. Don got really pissed when she referred to their evenings, and some afternoons, together as "booty calls."

Missy laughed at the memory as she headed down the short hall to her bedroom. By the time she washed up and brushed her teeth, Lady was curled up in the middle of her bed. Within minutes, Missy was in her pajamas and snuggled up next to the snoring cat. Soon, she was drifting off to sleep, her head full of sexy images of her absent lover.

It was a few months after her arrival on Mimosa Key when Missy first encountered the enigmatic artist. Levi asked her to stop by Don's gallery to pick up some paintings he had purchased for the office. She was a bit surprised Doc was buying art from a local, and—as best she could tell—virtually unknown artist. But since Levi paid her to take care of his dog, the renovation of his house, and any other details of his life he did not have the time or inclination to manage, she had said nothing. That morning she had signed for delivery of the Jaguar and made sure it was properly parked in Levi's newly constructed massive garage. She laughed as she pulled up in front of Don's building. It was typical of Levi that the garage was complete weeks before the renovation of the house, but he so loved his "toys"—as she was beginning to refer to them—she was not terribly surprised.

Her first impression of Don was that he had the darkest and saddest chocolate eyes she had ever seen. Her second impression was that he was truly a very talented artist. The series of four large seascapes that Levi had selected for the reception area of the new offices of FL-Ortho were stunning swirls and splashes of grey and white, depicting a stormy sea fighting torrential rain and wind. Missy had let out a low whistle of appreciation. She knew from personal experience with the waves off Cape Cod, that Don had perfectly captured the violence of a storm at sea. Then, she had laughed.

"Well, damn, they're magnificent. I just don't know if that is what I'd want to be staring at while I waited to hear if I was going to need a new knee or shoulder." Turning to Don, she added, almost apologetically, "But they are so amazing maybe patients will get lost in looking at them and forget to be scared...."

Her words were interrupted by an amused laugh from the painter. He shook his head as he stared at her. "Doc said you were a piece of work and he was right. But, don't tell him what you said. I don't want to have to refund his money if he changes his mind."

Don was wearing what she later realized was his usual outfit of paint-stained pants and ratty T-shirt. Thinking he needed the proceeds from the sale of the paintings, she just smiled when Levi had asked her what she thought of them. That had been the beginning of her friendship with Don. They complemented each other and shared a deep affection for Levi. They probably would have remained just friends, good friends, except for the intervention of tequila.

Earlier in the year, on a late spring night, Missy had been having a margarita at the Twisted Pelican with her friend and Yoga instructor, Libby Chesterfield, when a stranger, looking like some surfer dude, had approached her, claiming he knew her from somewhere. She had tried to put him off but he persisted, finally proposing a bet: if he could do five shots of tequila faster than Missy, she'd have to tell him who she really was. If he lost the bet, he'd pay for their drinks and leave them alone. Knowing her capacity for tequila and wanting to get rid of the guy, Missy took the bet. The surfer dude was good. Too good. The argument ensued when Missy had "accidentally" knocked over one of his shots. Rather than take the time to get a refill from the busy bartender, surfer dude had grabbed one of her shot glasses and downed the tequila. Missy had called foul and the stranger had gotten all up in her face.

"Now I'm sure I know you! Wherever it was that I saw you, you were being argumentative and sarcastic with some guy, just like now. A real bitch." His finger jammed the air in front of her nose.

Missy had been about to lunge at the guy and shut up his trash talk when Don had stepped between them.

He placed one hand on surfer dude's chest and the other on Missy's shoulder.

Before he could say a word, though, Libby's husband, Law Monroe, burst through the door of the kitchen and grabbed surfer dude by his collar. "You will apologize to the lady, now, or I will kick your sorry ass all the way to Naples. We don't allow that kind of language in front of our women." He started to drag the red-faced drunk out of the bar, calling over his shoulder, "Libby, honey, will you wait for me in the kitchen? And Don, can you make sure Missy gets home okay? Thanks, man."

Don's hand grasped Missy's elbow firmly, grabbed her purse from the back of the bar stool, then steered her toward the restaurant door. She had been fighting mad, mostly at the surfer dude who was about to blow her cover. Back in the day, she had occasionally appeared on the Washington political news shows and she'd been a tough opponent for some of the egotistical, condescending male talk show hosts. She *figured surfer dude had seen her on one of the shows and recognized her, though she was a good deal thinner and her hair was much longer now. But she was more than a little pissed at Don, who had stepped in like she was some weak-ass wimpy woman who could not take care of herself.*

"You can take your fucking hands off me any time, painter boy." She virtually snarled the words as they came out of the building and stepped into the parking lot. Missy was twisting her arm but Don was not letting go.

"I was comfortably ensconced in my booth at my favorite restaurant, quietly enjoying a plate of truly amazing lasagna, along with a glass of delicious Valpolicella, when what do I hear but loud voices coming from the bar. And who was it? You! I get up to investigate and what do I see but a feisty brunette nose-to-nose with a big, tanned, scruffy man." He actually shook her before he continued.

"You are going to come with me back to my building and I'm going to drive you home. Who knows if that figlio di puttana is still lurking about in an alley or side street just waiting for round two." He ground the words out, his hand like a vise on her arm.

She struggled with him down two streets and up the front steps of his building. He let go of her when they entered the foyer. She was sputtering mad.

"I don't need some guy dragging me around telling me what to do. You're not the boss of me!"

She gave him a shove, more out of embarrassment that she had used such a childish taunt than out of real anger. Astonishment and something else flashed across Don's face before he reached out and spun her around. She was up against the brick wall at the bottom of the stairway and he was pressed against her.

"Boss of you? Somebody sure needs to be the boss of you sometimes. What were you thinking getting into a barroom brawl with some drunk who was a foot taller and had at least a hundred pounds on you? That wise mouth of yours is going to get you into serious trouble someday."

"Well, it's my mouth and it's none of your business what I do with it." The words had no sooner escaped her lips when Don whipped her back around. He looked like he had been struck. They stood staring at each other, chests heaving, eyes flashing. Then his hands were buried in her hair and his tongue in her smart, reckless mouth.

It was like being engaged in a wrestling match. Hair pulling, teeth nipping, bodies grinding against each other. It had been three years since any man had touched her with desire—three years since she had been kissed. And no man had ever caressed her with such strong hands or devoured her mouth like Don. Missy did the only thing she could do in such a situation. She entwined her arms about his neck and hoisted her legs up and around his waist. He lifted his head to glare at her, his eyes as dark as bitter chocolate.

Within seconds, his hands cradled her ass and he carried her up to the second floor, all while his lips ravished hers. She heard her shoes fall off and clunk down the stairs. And she didn't care.

By the time Don got them into his bedroom, she had her hands under his faded gray sweatshirt, nails raking the long muscles on his back. His fingers were already fumbling with the button on her jeans. He dumped her on the bed and followed her down. They were naked in seconds, clothes flying all around the room as first one piece then another was removed and tossed in the air. Don rolled off her for a moment to curse unintelligibly. He rose and strode down the hall to the bathroom, emerging quickly with a handful of blue foil. Tossing the condoms on the bed, he grabbed one and ripped the wrapper open with his teeth. He looked at her with such intense longing, she was rendered virtually mute. His eyes never left her face as he covered his impressive erection. Easing down between her wide-stretched legs, he reached out to caress her face, gently, slowly.

"You sure about this, cara? You know this is dumb-ass crazy, but, God, I want you so bad." His voice shook with need.

"Yes," was all she could say. When he slid into her welcoming heat, her legs wrapped around him again, pressing him deep inside her. It was like nothing she had ever experienced before and it was every-

thing she had believed was only the made-up fantasies of romance writers. Her climax hit her so hard she saw stars and when she started giggling at her clichéd reaction to her first major orgasm, Don growled in her ear and redoubled his efforts. Moving over her, touching her everywhere as he stroked long and deep inside her, all Missy could do was hang on and gasp. Her second orgasm washed over her just as Don stopped moving. She felt him pulsing deep inside her and the clenching of his ass under her crossed ankles. When she wrapped her arms around him, her limp hands calmed the quivering muscles of his back as they both sucked in deep breaths.

Missy awoke the next morning alone in the tangled sheets. The smell of strong coffee cleared some of the tequila remnants from her brain. One eye opened carefully to the dim light of the bedroom, then widened at the sight of a steaming white mug on the table near the bed, next to it a croissant nestled a white cloth napkin. After wrapping herself toga style in the soft linen sheet, she ambled down the hall, coffee in one hand, pastry in the other.

Don was framed by the unadorned front windows, light pouring in around him as he stood studying the blank canvas on the easel. At the muffled sound of her bare feet on the polished wooden floor, he turned.

His tousled salt and pepper hair stood like a silver halo framing his head and mostly silver stubble shadowed his lean cheeks. As he assessed her naked shoulders, his bittersweet brown eyes seemed amused. And wary.

"Good croissant. Great coffee. Thank you." She raised the mug in salute.

"You're welcome. I stopped to get the croissants for us when I went out to move your car."

"You did what?" she squeaked, moving as quickly as she could to the front window to peer down on the still quiet street.

"I parked it the back so you could leave...undetected." His voice sounded uncertain.

"You don't want anyone to see me leave? What? You don't want

anyone to know you're fucking the housekeeper?" Her voice rose in anger.

"I don't give a rat's ass who sees you leave or who knows we shared my bed last night. I thought you might not want to do the 'walk of shame' over to the Twisted Pelican this morning or take a chance running into Bud wearing the same clothes he saw you in last night at the bar, when he opens his flower shop across the street in about twenty minutes. He's almost as big a gossip as Charity." His voice was still quiet, but had taken on a definite pissy tone. And for some reason that satisfied the bitchy, uncertain female who seemed to be currently residing inside her body.

"Okay, then." They just stared at each other until Missy took a loud noisy bite of the croissant.

Don's eyes narrowed when she stuck her tongue out to lick the crumbs off her lower lip.

Forty-five minutes later, Missy was driving back up to the North Shore with the windows down and the wind blowing through her still-damp hair. Shower sex with a horny artist was definitely the right way to start the morning. And a no-strings, mutually satisfying, additional benefit to being friends with Don Smith.

CHAPTER SIX

There was pain blossoming behind his eyes but it did not compare to the ache in his heart. Don finally emerged from his bedroom, still wearing his clothes from the day before. He stopped in the bathroom to pee and brush his teeth before he swallowed four aspirin with just a handful of water from the bathroom tap. The man staring at him from the mirror above the sink looked at least ninety, with bloodshot eyes and silver whiskers covering sunken cheeks. And a truly horrible case of bed hair.

"*Santa Maria, madre de Dio,*" he muttered as he faced the bright light in his main living space. A glance around the room told him most of the tale of the night before. An empty wine bottle stood on the kitchen counter and another was on the floor in front of the still open closet doors. A half-filled glass of red wine was precariously perched next to a paint-stained rag on the table next to his easel. The large canvas he had started less than twenty-four hours earlier rested on the easel, completed, except for his signature. He cautiously approached the painting. The deep undulating blue of the sea and the sky was bisected by a band of sunrise, colors emanating into the dawn and across the water from the pale yellow sun that was just emerging from the horizon. Stars fading in the heavens were reflected as diamonds dancing in the gentle waves. It was looser than most of his work, almost abstract, and it was brilliant.

Staring at the seascape he had no recollection of completing, his first impulse was to toss it across the room. He would not claim a painting when he had no idea how he had created it. His hands were reaching for the edges of the canvas, he was starting to turn toward the opposite wall, when something halted his movement. The light streaming in from the windows was reflecting off something, sending undulating rainbow prisms flitting around the room. His heart caught in his throat when he realized one of the rainbows danced across the last painting he had done of Gina and Raphael. Their two smiling faces were bathed in a kaleidoscope of color.

Gina had loved rainbows—they were her signature. She had talked him into painting a rainbow mural in Raphael's nursery, placing his crib right where the rainbow ended, explaining that their baby was their pot of gold. He had laughed at her; Gina had always been able to make him laugh, her sunny personality the perfect anti-dote for his sometimes-dark moods.

Surely it was a message from his lost love. She and his son were at peace. Great sobs wracked him as a huge weight lifted from his soul. Don wiped the tears from his eyes, his hands shaking. For so many years, he had wandered alone. For so many years, he had turned his back on love. And his work, while technically perfect, had lacked the inspiration that had made Donatello Stampone a sensation in the international art world. His portraits had been deemed luminous, visionary, and brilliant. The Vatican owned his Madonna and Child, painted with Gina and Raphael as the models. And he had walked away from his career and his fame the day he buried his wife and son on a cliff overlooking the Mediterranean.

Don could not bring himself to lock the painting back in the closet, to take the rainbow away from Gina and Raphael. He picked up the empty wine glass and bottle of Pinot Nero and headed to the kitchen. It was then that he realized the cascade of color was also washing over the seascape he had no memory of painting. The rainbow was like a blessing on the picture he had created for Missy. A blessing from Gina.

Too much emotion seeped through him. He left the empties on the kitchen counter and eased himself down on the overstuffed sofa in his "living room". For what seemed like hours, he sat and stared at the light and color filling the room, at the faces of his beloved wife and son. And at the beautiful scene that greeted him each morning when he left Missy's cottage.

After wandering around Europe and Asia, Don had made his way to North America. He'd traveled extensively in Canada and then settled briefly on the eastern shores of Mexico. A chance encounter with a couple he'd known in Italy who, thank God, had not recognized him, sent him packing. He had meandered along the Gulf Coast and the panhandle of Florida until he'd landed in Naples. But he did not want to stay. He'd attended art school in Naples, Italy and the memories were too strong for him to settle in a city with the same name. The area was recovering from a recent hurricane, especially the tiny island of Mimosa Key—just over the causeway from Naples. Almost the first thing he saw on the island was the battered white building facing the water, its blue shutters hanging askew. After making a few inquiries and one generous offer, the place was his.

Anxious to keep his identity hidden, he made arrangements with a bank in Miami Beach to handle the purchase and the modest renovations he planned. Don had no desire for anyone to realize he was Donatello Stampone, the up and coming portraitist who had disappeared from Italy years before. He transferred enough money from his account in Switzerland to cover his expenses; even with his years of travel he was still a wealthy man.

He had begun his life in Mimosa Key as a framer and occasional painter. Early on, he'd made friends with Clay and Lacey Walker. His seascapes had appealed to them as they were building and furnishing Casa Blanca Resort and Spa; the scenes were local, the paintings were huge, and the price was small. He didn't need the money so portraying himself as a small-time painter helped him maintain his alter-ego and kept a paintbrush in his hands. Even the mural he had created for Levi was not enough to bring him unwanted attention; it was just one more of Levi's quirks, embellishing his Hottie Rock Star image more than adding to Don's artistic reputation.

But then there was Missy.

She was everything Gina was not. Her dark hair, deep blue eyes, and impossibly long legs were totally at odds with his wife's petite blonde beauty, hazel eyes and musical voice. Missy spoke in tones of Lauren Bacall, deep and rough—her voice sometimes like sandpaper on his emotions. He had run into her numerous times at Levi's house, whenever there was a new vehicle to photograph so it could be memorialized on the wall of Levi's surgery or delivering framed canvases after Levi made another of his frequent forays into Don's shop to purchase one or two or five of Don's paintings for his home or office.

For years, Don had believed all he felt for Missy was casual affection. But, he could not ignore his growing respect for her organizational skills, her matter-of-fact approach to anything Levi or life threw at her, and her independent spirit. Not to mention her ability to get along with almost everyone on Mimosa Key—including Charity Grambling. It was almost as if the crotchety older woman had adopted her. Levi once opined that Charity had a major crush on him and she thought she could pump Missy to get the inside scoop on Levi's comings and goings.

"I try to stay on the old biddy's good side, Don, because she can make your life miserable if you cross her. But I do, really, respect her. She has built a business by herself and she doesn't take crap from anyone. That's not easy for a woman to do, even now, you know." Levi had raised a bottle of beer to Charity and toasted with Don in a booth at the South of the Border. "Kind of like Missy."

At Don's raised eyebrow, Levi had continued. "Well, you know, Missy arrived here shortly after me and not long, I think, after you settled here. When I met her, she had virtually nothing. But she stepped up to the plate, took over my life, and gave me the space and support I needed to build the practice and rebuild the house I bought. She's honest and hard-working and so damn capable she scares me. Missy's the real deal. I'd trust her with my life. Hell, I do trust her with my life!" He raised his bottle of beer to Missy before attacking another fish taco.

She was quite a woman. Don believed what Levi told him then and he had learned even more about the still mysterious brunette since he'd carried her up the stairs into his bedroom and into his life. He winced.

"Well, not really my life. She doesn't know anything about *me*—about Donatello Stampone." He glanced over at Gina's portrait again. The rainbows had disappeared, leaving her face bathed in the soft white light of the December morning. Another message?

"*Che cosa faccio adesso, il mio amore?* Do I trust her with our past, my lost darling? Do I put my future into her very capable hands? *Quel che sarà sarà.* What will be, will be."

CHAPTER SEVEN

---

*Y*ou saved my life with lunch/dinner yesterday! I apologize for not thanking you sooner but I was painting...and selling almost everything in the shop to Clay. Can I make it up to you with dinner tonight? I want you.

Missy looked over at the message on her phone. Finally. She had been feeling a little pissed off at Don—not for being incommunicado for over 24 hours, but for not letting her know he liked her eggplant parm. She knew how particular he was about red sauce. She couldn't respond right off—and he could wait a few minutes after making her wait for a whole day—because her hands were buried deep in a chicken carcass. She was still feeling a bit off and the weather had a definite chill to it so she'd decided that a nice chicken soup for dinner would fit the bill. And leave her with enough cooked chicken to make a ton of chicken salad for Levi's and Ella's lunches tomorrow and the next day. They were addicted to chicken salad. Especially hers.

Great idea, she had thought, until she was faced with pulling apart two boiled chickens. Her iffy stomach was roiling around at the sight of bones and skin, something that had never bothered her before. *Damn, this really might be a stomach bug. If I'm not feeling better tomorrow, I'll go see the doctor.* She needed to get into town to the bank, in any event. Her quarterly inheritance check had been deposited on December first and she needed to move some money around in her account. She didn't like leaving a trail on the Internet, so every few months she drove up the coast to Clearwater and did her banking, a little shopping, and sometimes took in a baseball game— especially during Spring Training.

"I've got enough chicken here for an army, Hersch. Good thing you and Lady Marmalade will eat the scraps." She dropped a handful of skin and bits in the Lab's bowl. It was gone in an instant and he was nudging her for more. "No," she said, reaching for a small plastic bag, "this is for Lady."

Hersch went over to lie in front of the patio doors and sulk, while Missy finished dividing the chicken between the pot full of broth and fresh vegetables and a plastic container which would soon hold chicken salad. She contemplated making matzoh balls but her stomach turned over again at the thought of beating eggs. "Noodles it is, then." Within moments, the chicken and egg noodle soup was complete and the kitchen set to rights. Missy paused long enough in her routine to text a quick message to Don.

I'm not up for dinner tonight but stop by and I'll share some home-made chicken noodle soup with you. I've been wanting you, too.

She'd barely made it down the hall to the laundry room when her cellphone beeped again.

Are you tired or sick? Can I bring you something or would you like to be alone? I could kiss whatever is bothering you and make it better.

A few more text exchanges, while Missy put one load of laundry in the dryer and started another washing, set their evening plans for soup and saltines at seven, with Don bringing diet ginger ale. By mid-afternoon she was feeling better—so good that she made two apple pies, one for Doc and Ella and one for her and her lover.

Just before seven, Hersch's barking from Levi's front porch announced Don's impending arrival. His Jeep was pulling into the parking space next to her cottage just as she opened the front door.

After a quick cleaning of her own place, she'd taken a warm shower and washed her long brown hair. She loved the lavender scent of the shower gel and matching shampoo Ella had given her on her last birthday. Knowing that her bra and panties were the same silky hue as the fragrance and the light sweater she wore had her smiling secretively as Don climbed out of the Jeep. The man was in for a surprise. He loved peeling sexy underwear off her, although occasionally, he moved so fast that clasps were broken and elastic torn. But he always replaced it on his next visit.

Damn, he looked good. And different. He's changed since I saw him last...but how? Same tousled salt and pepper hair, a little damp from a recent shower. Good, she thought, he probably used that evergreen eucalyptus blend of soap and shampoo he favored. It reminded her of a long-ago trip to Tuscany. And he'd shaved. *Mmmm*, she felt herself getting damp because she knew that when this man shaved, she'd eventually be feeling the silky glide of his cheeks brushing against her inner thighs.

Don flashed her a blinding smile before he turned to get something from the passenger seat. He produced a fabric tote bag with the top of a soda bottle peeping out, next to the long green neck of a bottle of wine. And flowers. Daisies. How did he know she loved daisies? Within moments, he swept her into an embrace, something he usually waited to do until they were inside the cottage. No public displays of affection was their rule. His lips brushed her forehead while his arms remained wrapped around her, the tote bag dangling from his wrist banging against her butt.

"Good, you're not running a temperature. I was worried about you. Charity just told me that there's been a particularly nasty bit of stomach flu going around, lots of kids missing school. She thinks its food poisoning from what she is sure was bad turkey served at the Mimosa Key Thanksgiving Feast. Always looking on the bright side, that one."

Missy laughed as he released her and held the door open. "Charity is a real conspiracy theorist, you know. I'm surprised she doesn't think some drone dropped poison on all of us. But, I'm feeling much better now, so I don't think its food poisoning."

He moved to put the bag on the kitchen counter, pulling the bouquet out and presenting it to her with a flourish. "My mother always said daisies were perfect for a sick visit because they were like little smiling faces. And everyone loves daisies."

Missy accepted the bouquet with a small curtsey. "Your mother is a very smart woman. I love daisies, whether I'm ill or not."

Don paused in removing the wine and ginger ale from the bag. He stood still for a moment, just looking at her. "Was. My mother *was* a wise woman. She passed away some time ago." And then he shrugged as if her passing and his sharing were of no import.

Missy laid a hand on his arm, on the sleeve of a surprisingly unstained black T-shirt.

He glanced over at her with a quizzical look.

"I'm sorry your mom died. I didn't know." She swallowed and paused, as he had, considering what to say, what to share next. "My mother is dead. She died shortly before I moved here."

They just stared at each other, the confidences they had shared weaving silken strands of intimacy around them, the sheer volume of their unspoken secrets making the air heavy with emotion. Don moved first. His artist's hand, graceful but rough, reached out to stroke her cheek, his calloused thumb brushing away the single tear that threatened to spill from her eye. For an instant, she leaned her cheek into his hand and her eyes drooped closed, savoring the intimacy, accepting the gesture.

Before her eyes could open, his other hand had clasped hers and he pulled her into his arms. As soon as his lips brushed hers, the always banked embers of their desire burst into flames. Missy's arms swept around his waist, her hands tunneling up under his shirt, her nails raking the long smooth muscles of his workingman's back. His tongue invaded her mouth, as his fingers swept up into her hair, imprisoning her head in his gentle grip.

They ravaged each other's mouths, nipping and moaning, teeth clicking against teeth, tongues tangling, pausing to gulp air, each breath coming out hot and fast, before they dove into the depths of passion again.

Don pulled away first, gasping. His eyes were wild. "Where? Here?" His hands were cupping her ass as he lifted her against him. All Missy could think was that she wanted him inside her now. Her tush plopped down on the counter. Don was tugging at the drawstring on her dark green pants. He got it loose and yanked the slacks down from her waist. They were almost off her ankles when he looked up from the lavender silk triangle at the apex of her thighs.

"*Madre de Dio*," he muttered. "You're killing me." Missy felt the warm flush of feminine satisfaction wash over her.

He laid her gently down across the counter, her head mere inches from where he'd left the bottles of wine and soda, her pants dangling from one foot. His work-roughened hands pushed her sweater up and over her shoulders. Don groaned as he touched her breasts, spilling from the silk cups of the lavender bra. She arched her back under his stroking, his hands working until her nipples were achingly hard. With his fingers still caressing her torso, his face lowered between her legs. He used his aristocratic nose to nudge aside the silken scrap of her panties. "*Bellisima*," he muttered, one land leaving her breast to yank the panties away from her center. He breathed deeply, she could feel the hot air from his lungs caressing her core. Now both of his hands were spreading her thighs, pushing the silk away, fingers sliding into her as he opened her wide.

"God, I love the way you smell—almost as much as I love how you taste." Then those clever, clever fingers were inside her and his tongue... *Oh, my God...* his tongue was lapping at her. Moaning, she started thrusting, while his mouth made love to her. Missy felt herself lose her mind and lose control. Then the lights behind her eyes exploded. She heard herself scream before she went limp. But Don did not lift his head until she came again.

The air in the cottage was thick with the smell of sex, lavender, and pine. And chicken soup. Missy levered herself up on her elbows.

Don's head rested on his crossed arms, draped across her thighs. She reached out a shaky hand to stroke his disheveled salt and pepper hair. Looking up, his dark eyes met hers. A smile twitched his lips, then his deep laugh filled the small space.

"Well, I said I would kiss whatever was bothering you and make it better." His eyes strayed to her crotch and he grinned. "I hope that worked for you."

"You're off by several inches, Romeo, but I could have a compound fracture and I'd still feel great after that...*kiss*. Help me get down and I'll dish us up some soup. I'm starving." As if to prove it, her stomach growled.

Don scooped her up then let her slide down his hard length until her bare feet hit the tile floor.

As she bent to drag panties and pants back up her legs, she stopped to stare at the bulge in his jeans. After planting a noisy kiss in the general area of his fly, she straightened. "I'm sorry I can't take care of what's bothering you now, but I need to turn that soup off and get the rolls I baked out of the warming drawer. Can you wait 'til after we eat?"

"I've already eaten, thank you." Don continued to laugh at her, especially when she wiggled by him and stuck out her tongue.

As Missy served the soup and rolls, Don poured them each a glass of Vinho Verde. It seemed to her that there was a new ease to their relationship. And a new depth. *Where had that come from?*

Missy placed the soup bowls on the counter and turned to retrieve spoons and napkins. Don was already sitting on a stool, pulling one of the warm rolls apart and making sounds of gustatory anticipation. *It's like he belongs here.* With her back still to him, words spilled swiftly from Missy's lips.

"I'm an orphan. My father died just before my mother. I don't have any siblings. Or children. It's just me."

The knife Don had been using clattered to the marble surface of the counter, striking an almost musical note. Missy turned back to him at the sound but then froze in place, the stricken look on his face making her wait for him to speak.

"I'm an orphan, too. And an only child." He took a gulp of wine, as if to give himself strength. And to steal a few minutes before he finished responding, his voice very low. "And I don't have any children either."

"Okay, then," Missy said as she placed the spoons and napkins on the counter and sat on the stool next to him. Their thighs brushed. Again, she felt flushed, especially when Don reached over and squeezed her leg, gently, his thumb finishing with a swirling caress.

"Okay, then." He turned his attention to the soup, the tension on his face eased.

Conversing about the work they'd accomplished over the past day, they passed a companionable hour, savoring soup and sipping wine.

"I've gotten several of the paintings matted and framed but I'm running out of the specific mat I've used in the past for Casa Blanca artwork. I'm going to need to head over to Miami." Don finished the wine in his glass. "Would you like to go for a ride with me...maybe day after tomorrow?"

Missy just stared at him. They had never really gone anywhere or done anything together. Sure, they might meet for fish tacos at the SOB or have a beer at the Twisted Pelican. They had even had some meals with Levi and Ella at the main house during the past few months —especially when Levi was attempting to grill. But never a date.

"Well, I want to dig out Hanukkah decorations tomorrow for the inside of the main house. I've already arranged for the landscape guys to be here early on Monday to lay down more crushed shells on the drive, clean up some of the debris from the last storm, and refresh the planters. I need to pick up office supplies for Ella and do a major Post Office run. I can do that anywhere. Yeah, a trip to Miami works out just fine for me. Assuming you're buying me lunch at some funky food truck on Miami Beach before we head back here."

"Woman, you are too easy. Lunch from a food truck? You got it." Don rose to clear the dishes. His innate neatness was one of the qualities she liked about him. And his assumption that if she cooked, he would clean up. His graceful efficient movements in her kitchen and the fact that he knew without being told where everything went brought a smile to her face.

Don looked over at her and stopped putting dishes in the dishwasher. "What's that goofy grin for?"

"You look good in my...the...kitchen. Levi always looks a bit out of place, even in that huge, high-tech kitchen of his. For that matter, so does Ella." She laughed. "But, you fit in this little kitchen perfectly." She raised her glass to toast him with the swallow of wine that was left.

Don brought the wine bottle over to where she sat, dividing what remained into their two glasses. He lifted his glass to her. "Missy, this little cottage is the perfect frame for you. You fill every room with your spirit. *Bella*, every place you go, you bring warmth and humor. You fit in everywhere you go. *Saluti!*" He touched his glass to hers and took a deep sip of wine.

"Don," she started to speak then stopped. They never asked any questions about their pasts; their relationship was strictly in the present. But, the evening had already revealed so much they had not known about each other, that she felt emboldened to continue. "Don, maybe I never noticed before, but you seem to use a lot of Italian expressions. Is...was...your family Italian?"

He stepped away from her, his laughing face suddenly a blank mask. His eyes darted around the small cottage, as if looking for an avenue of escape. He stood very still for an instant, as if he was listening for a sound from afar. Then, with a small shake of his shoulders, his gentle smile returned.

"Yes, I'm Italian. I mean, I was born in Italy. My father was Italian but my mother was American. She met my father during a summer abroad to visit relatives in Italy after college and married him. We visited her family in New York once in a while, but mostly, they came to the old country to spend summers with us." He shrugged. "We need more wine."

"There's a bottle of Moscato in the wine rack." Missy gestured to the small shelf between the kitchen and the living room. While Don busied himself with the cork screw, Missy digested what he had shared with her. Don had told her more this evening than she had learned from him in all the years they'd known each other. Maybe it was time for her to do the same. She had been sleeping with him for almost nine months and she had told him nothing of herself, really, beyond her preferences in food and wine. And sex.

He placed a glass in front of her and leaned against the counter, taking an appreciative sip of the sweet golden wine.

"My parents were born in France. My mother was Jewish and she lost most of her family in the war. My father was Catholic. They met after university, married, and then emigrated to Boston. I grew up in Boston."

"I wondered. You have an unusual accent sometimes when you're tired or really excited. I thought it sounded like New England but there's a little something else. I'll bet you were...are...fluent in French."

"*Mais oui.*" She sipped the wine as her mind raced. Should she tell him she also spoke several other languages? No, this was enough for one night. Missy set her glass down and came around the counter to Don. Running her hands up his well-muscled chest, she crooned the words of the La Belle hit song from the 1970's.

"*Voulez vous coucher avec moi?*" She ended with a quick nip on his lower lip.

Don responded in an ancient and universal language by sweeping Missy into his arms and carrying her down the hall to her bedroom. After dumping his lover on the bed, he scooped up her surprised orange and white cat and placed her in the hall. And shut the door in her startled feline face.

CHAPTER EIGHT

True to form, Missy pulled Levi's Volvo into Don's back parking area at seven o'clock sharp on Monday morning. He was just walking down the steps from the shop as she got out of the car, purse slung over her shoulder, tote bag in one hand, and a travel mug of lemon ginger tea in her other. Her stomach was still slightly queasy though not as bad as it had been during the past week. She felt better but she'd actually applied a little blush to hide the pallor of her cheeks.

"We're going shopping for stuff, Missy. Why are you bringing stuff with us?" Don reached for the tote bag.

"I made us breakfast burritos and I packed some granola bars I made yesterday. And there's a travel cup of really strong coffee for you in there, too." His face lit up with a grin as he rummaged around in her bag and pulled out the stainless-steel mug.

"Mmmm. Just the way I like it. This saves me a stop at the Super Min. So double thank you for bringing me goodies and sparing me an early morning encounter with Charity."

They made themselves as comfortable as possible in Don's old

Jeep and headed off Mimosa Key over the causeway to Naples. The drive to Miami took a little over two hours. Don consumed two of the breakfast sandwiches and a granola bar, while all Missy could manage was half of her plain egg burrito and most of her hot tea.

"What is it with men? It's so not fair. You eat all that stuff and you don't gain an ounce. I eat an extra cookie and I can't close my jeans." Missy was grumbling as she tucked the remainder of her sandwich back in the tote. Don just laughed at her.

"What are you concerned about? You're as long and leggy as a spring colt. There's not an extra pound on you anywhere. Not that I'd care if there was. You must know what a beautiful woman you are." He glanced over at her. "Right? You are *bellisima*."

A faint flush stained her cheeks. "Well, thank you. It's hard to feel beautiful this early in the morning. This little trip is a nice change to my routine but, damn, it was hard to put mascara on while it was still dark outside!"

"I appreciate the effort but you didn't have to go to any trouble for me. And we're just running some errands and grabbing lunch at a food truck. It's not like we're dining at the Ritz Carlton."

"Well, you're wearing a regular shirt and clean khakis and real shoes, so I could hardly join you in my grey sweatshirt and holey jeans, with my hair in a ponytail and no make-up." She'd put on black leggings and black flats to go with the indigo trapeze sweater she wore, a black and indigo scarf twined around her slender neck. Her long dark hair swung around her shoulders in silken strands and silver hoops danced from her ears.

"Like I said, *bellisima!*" Don reached over to trail his fingers down her cheek. "You look just perfect for a day trip to Miami."

"So, tell me, why don't you just use a bank in Naples? Why do you go to Miami to do your banking? If you don't mind me asking...."

Don sighed deeply, his fingers drumming nervously on the steering wheel. A few very quiet moments elapsed before he spoke, moments that made Missy squirm uncomfortably in her seat.

"Well, as I told you, I was born in Italy. I lived there until about twelve years ago. I decided to travel and I needed an international bank. There isn't one in Naples but there is a branch in Miami of one I have used elsewhere. When I settled in Mimosa Key a few years ago, I wanted a bank in Florida to handle the purchase of my building, so I opened an account in Miami. It's not a bad drive, gets me away from Mimosa Key once in a while, and my favorite art supply store is located not far from my bank, so I usually combine banking and restocking in one trip."

Missy nodded her head. She had a similar situation that she was not quite ready to share. She, too, used a bank away from Naples—a bank with branches all over the country. Her infrequent vacation time away from Mimosa Key always included a trip to a different city; one in which a branch of her bank was located. She did not just have an inheritance to manage; the buy-out from her firm, the proceeds of the sale of her townhouse in Georgetown and its contents and the money she had invested over the years when she was commanding a six-figure salary in DC had made her a very wealthy woman. Not quite Levi and Ella and Fitz level of wealthy, but enough so that she did not really need to ever work again. Given Don's description of his banking needs, it dawned on her that perhaps he was not the struggling artist everyone seemed to think he was. Maybe she was not the only one with deep, dark secrets.

When they arrived in Miami, they stopped first at Don's bank. Missy waited in the Jeep, enjoying the cool breeze off the ocean and watching the people on the crowded city street. She did not miss the hustle and bustle of living in a city, the fast pace of her former life in the nation's capital. "Just the shoes, sometimes," she thought as she admired the pair of bright blue stilettos a leggy young woman was teetering in as she maneuvered her way through the cross-walk. *Those are Jimmy Choo's. I'd bet my bank account on it.* She turned to follow the woman's progress and saw Don emerging from the bank, an intent look on his handsome face.

The rest of the morning passed quickly. They were both efficient shoppers, organized and decisive. After taking Missy to a large post office and an even larger office supply store to get everything she needed for Ella and Levi's home offices, Don pulled into the lot of Jerry's Artarama.

"I'm only taking an hour here. Time me. I've been known to spend the whole day in art supply stores." When she saw the size of the list he pulled up on his phone, she believed him. Armed with two shopping carts, they speedily made their way through paints, mats, and canvases. It was not until Don stopped in front of a display of Kolinsky sable brushes that their timetable began to fall apart. While Missy gasped at the prices, Don lovingly caressed the fine silky brushes then gently placed them in his cart. There were at least a dozen when Missy reminded him of the time.

Later, they enjoyed fabulous grilled cheese sandwiches at the Ms. Cheezious food truck. Relaxing in the adjacent patio, Missy found herself once again plying Don with questions.

"How often do you need to restock at places like Jerry's? The Jeep is almost full to its ragtop with supplies." What she was really asking him was how he could afford to drop over two thousand dollars on brushes alone.

"I needed more stuff than I usually do because Clay pretty much cleaned me out last week. I'll need to paint at least a dozen canvases just to cover the empty spaces in the gallery. And I needed some acrylics for Levi's mural." At her arched brow, he explained the painting he was doing for Ella as her Hanukkah present for Levi. "I know you won't say anything because it's supposed to be a surprise for the first night."

A low whistle was her response. "Wow, you're going to have to hustle. The first night of Hanukkah is in eight days. Levi usually operates on Monday, Wednesday and Friday. How are you going to make it happen?"

"Ella checked his schedule and he's not operating that Monday. So, I'll paint the mural this coming Saturday and Sunday. It will be dry and there will be no paint fumes when she shows it to him Tuesday night."

"He'll love it. A hot red Mustang, Ella and Hersch. His three favorites. What more could he ask for?"

"How about you? What do you want for Hanukkah this year, little girl?" Don gave her a crazy Santa leer.

She was silent. She had never really celebrated the holiday. Her mother tended to ignore celebrations and her father was Catholic. It had not been until she moved to Levi's property that Missy had gotten into looking forward to holidays.

"Hmmm. I would have said nothing before today. But I'm still having shoe envy over those blue Jimmy Choo high heels I saw on a leggy blonde outside your bank." At his surprised look, she added mischievously, "And a rhinestone collar for Lady Marmalade. This little fluffy dog was wearing one this morning and I thought how Lady would look so glamorous in one." Don was still staring at her so she punched him in the arm to let him know she was just kidding. She didn't expect anything from him. It's not like he was her boyfriend.

"I'm not used to anyone buying me gifts. Levi does every year for my birthday and Hanukkah but except for holiday gift exchanges with my girlfriends at Yoga class and soap-making class, I'm not really into the whole gift thing." Don reached out to touch her hand, then he raised it to his lips for a tender kiss. A kiss that made her melt and made her uncomfortable. There was more than just lust in his eyes, she was sure of it. There was affection. But how could he have feelings for her when he didn't really know her?

"I don't need presents." She just blurted it out. Don raised his lips from her hand but did not let go of it. "I mean, sure, everyone likes presents, but I don't need people to give me things. Levi keeps trying to give me a car, even though he and I are both fine with me just driving whichever of his is available since most of the time I'm driving somewhere for him. Or for Ella."

This was not going the way she wanted it to. She was trying to tell Don something about herself and he just looked more confused. And amused.

"I have a bank account in Clearwater. Well, Tampa, really, but when I go up there, I usually hang out in Clearwater, because of the beach and all. But I think I know why you come here to bank because I go off Mimosa Key to bank too. It's because I don't want anyone to know too much about me. Well, Levi and Ella know some stuff, but I don't want people from my past showing up."

"Are you in some kind of trouble, Missy? Are you running from the law?" Don's voice sounded shocked—as if he couldn't imagine that she would ever do anything illegal.

"No, nothing like that. I walked away from a job I no longer needed and a man I no longer loved, if I ever loved him, which I doubt. I don't want to ever have to deal with those people again."

His dark eyebrows crooked up. In astonishment or was it abhorrence?

She took a long sip of water to buy herself some time. She'd heard that confession was good for the soul, but right now she felt like hell. "It's just that I have a lot of money. I'm not saying that to brag or show off to you. It's just that, well, you have this bank account here in Miami because you need an international bank, which says to me that you have money abroad that you need to be able to access. And you spent way more at the art supply store today than I figure a struggling artist would be able to pay out for paintings that had not been commissioned yet. And you asked me what I wanted for the holidays. So, I felt I should tell you that you don't have to worry that I'd be interested in you because you probably have money because I have money, too. That's all."

A slow smile spread across his face and then he gathered her into his arms, muttering some beautiful Italian words into her hair. Don held her there in the little courtyard, as winter sun cast dappled shadows on the ground and people chattered around them. Then, he pulled back a little from her, his sable eyes burning into hers.

"You are a wonder. I adore you. I must because as much as I love making love to you I think I may love just listening to you almost as much. You fascinate me, *cara*. Why did it take me so long to realize it?" He bent to kiss her. Before his lips brushed hers, he whispered, "I'm really, really rich."

CHAPTER NINE

On the drive home from Miami, they held hands. Except when Don had to shift gears, but as soon as his hand left the stick, he reached for Missy again. Now that the dark secret of her finances had come to light, words spilled out of her. She told him about her upbringing in Boston and her rise to wealth and power in Washington. She would not tell him the name of the man who had betrayed her trust—which was probably just as well because Don had an overwhelming urge to pummel him until he was unrecognizable.

For his part, Don revealed some of his secrets. But not his real name and nothing about Gina and Raphael. He explained, truthfully, that he had become disenchanted with the international art scene, and had decided to travel extensively, seeking new inspiration. It was a lot to take in, he knew. By the time they crossed the Causeway, Missy's head was nodding with fatigue.

He brought her to his building and helped her up the stairs, telling her she should nap for a few hours, before she headed home to the North Shore. Don barely had time to tuck a soft coverlet around Missy after slipping off her shoes, before she was snuffling softly, as she did when she was deep asleep. He spent the next two hours unpacking his Jeep and stowing away all his new supplies. The seascape he had painted for Missy had been locked in the closet, guarded by Gina and Raphael.

The sun was starting to sink into the Gulf when Missy's footsteps on the stairs announced she was awake. Don looked up from the canvas he was framing to see her stretching and yawning in the doorway of the gallery.

"Hey, Sleeping Beauty, you don't look like you're quite awake yet. Do you want to sleep some more? You could stay over."

"Hmmm, no, but thank you. I need to get Levi's car back, though I'm sure he won't be needing it. And I really must see to Lady Marmalade. So, I should be going. Did you leave my stuff in your Jeep?" She looked around for her tote and purse. And her shopping bags.

"Yes, but I locked the Jeep. Come on and I'll help you move your loot to Levi's car." He grabbed his keys from the table and walked with her down the hall to the back door. It took just a few minutes to transfer Missy's things to the Volvo. She was getting ready to slide into the driver's seat when Don reached for her. His arms wrapped around her as his lips found hers. He felt his heart move as she sighed into his mouth, desire pooling in his gut as their tongues tangled.

He let her go with the promise that he would come to her that night, late because he had work to do for Clay and Lacey.

It was dark when he drove north later that evening, stopping first at Casa Blanca to drop off several more framed paintings at Lacey's office. The lights were out in the main house when he pulled down the white shell drive to park next to Missy's cottage. Lady Marmalade was waiting for him just inside the door, meowing softly. He bent to pet her regal head, thinking that Missy had been right—a rhinestone collar was just what the cat needed. He poured some cream in her bowl then made his way down the short hall to Missy's room. Music was softly playing, but not in the bedroom. Soft lights flickered from the en suite. The sight that he beheld when he pushed open the door to the bathroom would be etched in his mind forever,

In a tub almost overflowing with bubbles, her head laying back against a blue terry pillow, her hair piled up with strands escaping from a messy top knot, shadowed eyes closed, with just the tops of her breasts visible through the soapy water, was the dark-haired beauty who was worming her way into his heart. Adele was singing her heart out about broken hearts and Missy was humming along, lost in the song. Don pulled his shirt over his head and dropped it on the floor, his jeans were next, then his boxers completed the soft pile of clothing. Carefully, he stepped into the tub, facing her, but there was no way for him to slide beneath the bubbles without disturbing her.

"What took you so long?" Her blue eyes opened in amusement and he realized she had probably known he was there all along. Then, her eyes widened at the sight of his throbbing arousal. She slid upright, making room for him to ease down into the water opposite her, exposing the deep pink crests of her breasts, already tightened into hard buds. As soon as he was in the water, he reached for her, his hands sliding over and under and around, stroking her silky skin. Her eyes never left his face. His hands slid down to her hips and he pulled her forward, until she was kneeling over him, her knees hugging his thighs. She rose up, then gently lowered herself onto him, taking every rock-hard inch of him inside her. Unable to resist, he leaned forward, her ass cupped in his hands, and licked the drops of water off her nipples. A ragged indrawn breath let him know how much she wanted him to taste her. His tongue played with her as she settled herself to her task: to ride him into ecstasy. Small waves rose around them and caressed them every time she moved. He knew he was about to explode and wanted her with him. His fingers traced the separation between the cheeks of her butt. As soon as he touched her, she clenched around his hard, throbbing length, drawing every drop from him as they came together.

Later, as they lay together in Missy's bed, drifting off to sleep for the first time in each other's arms, he heard her whisper against his chest, "I love you." Don's arms tightened around her, pulling her even closer. His lips pressed to her silken hair, "*Ti amo*. I love you, too."

Missy was curled into a tight ball on the edge of the bed, wrapped up in the comforter like one of her breakfast burritos, when Don awoke to a raspy tongue licking his hand that was draped off the side of the bed. Staring down into Lady's demanding green eyes, he silently warned her to be quiet. Like so many mornings when he had awakened before Missy, he eased quietly from the bed, determined to let his lover sleep. He found his clothes in the bathroom, thankfully still dry despite the water that had sloshed over the sides of the claw foot tub where they had made love the night before. Dressing and brushing his teeth by the faint light of sunrise filtering through the bathroom curtains, Don couldn't stop grinning.

Even putting up with Lady's demands to be fed and petted did not dampen his good mood. *Great mood*, he corrected himself as he climbed into his Jeep. It was going to be a great day. The sky was almost as beautiful as it had been the morning he'd begun Missy's seascape. He had money in the bank, work he was born to do, and a damn fine woman who loved him. All was right in his world.

CHAPTER TEN

Missy waited until she heard Don start up his Jeep and pull away from her cottage, the crunch of the tires on the seashell driveway fading, before she sat up. Dizziness swept over her, almost forcing her to crawl back under the covers. She sat there, legs dangling, her head buried in her hands, waiting for nausea to pass. The urge to pee finally drove her into the bathroom, where she was promptly sick. Rather than go back to bed, Missy decided to tough it out, get cleaned up and head over to the main house. The woman looking back from the mirror while she brushed her teeth had dark circles under her eyes, a faint sheen of perspiration on her brow and cheekbones that were sharper than they had ever been before.

What the hell is wrong with me? "You know, Lady," she almost whined to the cat who had stayed by her side throughout her travail, "it would be just my luck now that I have finally met a man I can love, to find out I have some horrible disease." Recalling the whispered declarations of love from the night before brought a smile to her lips and butterflies to her stomach. Her left hand strayed down to her tummy, to calm the flutters she felt as she recalled Don's husky voice whispering that he loved her in Italian and English. The words were sweet in any language but she hugged *"ti amo"* to her heart.

Then she froze. Missy stared in the mirror at her left hand, resting on the slight mound of her stomach. No, make that her nicely rounded abdomen. She lifted up her nightshirt to stare at what was definitely a bulge She had never had six-pack abs but she'd been damn close. Now that she was looking, it was obvious that she had put on weight in her stomach area. Over her shoulder in the mirror's reflection, she saw the claw foot tub. She blushed as images of the night before scrolled through her memory. A slight smile played around her lips but the word that slipped out was "damn."

They hadn't used a condom! Damn, she'd been so caught up in how sexy her man had looked getting naked and stepping into the tub with her, she'd almost come when his hands stroked over her breasts. She'd just climbed right up onto his lap and sunk down on his beautiful hard cock without a thought in the world about birth control. What if she was pregnant? She shivered as though someone had dumped a tub of ice water all over her, like those Facebook challenges from a year ago.

No, wait. Stupid girl. Don't jump to conclusions. You didn't get pregnant last night. Your tummy wouldn't be sticking out even a tiny bit if you just got pregnant last night. She almost laughed at herself, at her foolishness, but before she could sigh with relief, harsh facts slammed into her brain. *I can't remember when my last period was.* She yanked open the linen closet door. There, stashed behind a four-pack of toilet paper, was an unopened box of tampons. *Think!* It was usually the third week of the month. November. Thanksgiving week. So busy, with Levi's family in town and the Annual Mimosa Key Thanksgiving Festival. Nope, she didn't have a period then. When? October? She couldn't remember. Damn!

Reeling back into her bedroom, she threw on underwear, jeans, and a sweatshirt, and slipped her feet into her moccasins. Grabbing the keys to the Volvo and her purse, she dashed out the door, pausing only to bend down to where Lady Marmalade was curled on her favorite chair in the early morning light and whisper, "Oh, Lady, what are we going to do?"

Missy drove over the causeway to Naples, then headed north until she came across a suburban strip mall with a pharmacy. She wandered up and down every aisle twice to make sure there was no one from Mimosa Key, no one she even remotely knew, anywhere in the store. Her cart was full of stuff she blindly picked off the shelves. Ladies razors. Mouthwash. Shampoo. Cat food. Red licorice. And three pregnancy tests. She paid cash to the disinterested young clerk and then dumped the bags in the trunk of the car.

By the time she pulled into the carport next to Levi's and Ella's house, it was after eight o'clock. "I can't do this alone." She glanced over at the front door. Levi would already be in surgery. Ella was probably up and in her office. Missy took everything out of the bag the tests were in except the red licorice and climbed the stairs to the front porch. She let herself in to the sound of Hersch's excited barks. But the big dog was not sitting by the door. Missy followed the sounds into the kitchen where she found Ella removing a breakfast burrito from the microwave.

"Hey, Missy. I didn't expect you until nine. What's up? You want one of these egg and cheese thingies or do you want one with sausage? Hersch will probably fight you for it, though. Poor baby is starving after our run on the beach this morning." Ella continued talking while she took her plate and a mug of coffee over to the stools at the island and sat down. "How was your trip with Don yesterday? Did you have a good time? Hey, did you get me some more ink cartridges? I need to print..." The author's voice trailed off as she realized that Missy had not moved and had not spoken. "Are you okay?" Ella rose and went to her friend, pulling Missy to over to sit next to her. "You're as pale as a ghost. Let me make you some lemon and ginger tea. Maybe a piece of toast." When Missy started to rise, Ella placed a hand on her shoulder to make her sit. "Stop. I can do it. Even *I* can make a piece of toast." She glanced down at the white plastic shopping bag clenched in Missy's hands. "What's this? I see red licorice. Yay! I ran out late yesterday and I'm going to need it if I plan on writing anything today."

When Ella moved to take the bag. Missy clutched it to her chest. "It's not licorice. I mean, it's not *just* licorice." Her hands opened and the contents of the bag spilled out onto the counter. Ella's eyes flew open and her mouth made a perfect "O". Then she wrapped Missy in a two-armed hug and rocked her as Missy began to cry.

"I was going to ask if this means good news or bad news. I can't tell if your tears are tears of joy or regret."

Missy swiped her eyes with her sleeve and laughed shakily. "They're tears of abject terror." She related to Ella what had happened earlier that morning, even joining the other woman in her laughter about Missy assuming her stomach was sticking out because she had gotten pregnant the night before.

"Well, I have no experience with being pregnant, as you now know, though I have tons of experience with wanting to be. You don't look like you want to be."

"I'm not sure what I want. Twenty-four hours ago, I would have said pregnancy was the last thing on my mind—the most remote possibility in the world and something I would avoid at all costs. I was living a quiet and satisfying, though secretive, life, with an excellent lover on the side. Now, I've discovered my lover has some secrets of his own. But, I know he loves me. And I know I love him. That's all I know. Except I'm pretty damn sure I'm pregnant at almost forty."

"Well, we know that happens, we've seen evidence of it here in Bare-foot Bay. Hell, you said your own mother got pregnant with you when she was in her mid-forties. Nothing to be ashamed of or to really worry about, with all the advances in pre-natal care. But," Ella gave Missy another fierce hug, "we're getting worried about the verdict before all the evidence is in. Time for you to go pee and find out if you're knocked up, girlfriend."

She used all three kits. The results were lined up in a neat row on the vanity in the powder room. Missy and Ella stared at the indicators. One had two pink lines for positive, one showed the word "yes" and the third simply said "pregnant" in the tiny message window. Ella pointed to the last strip and said, "That's my favorite. I think we should frame that one."

Missy leaned against the older woman, who she had come to love like a big sister. "You think this is good news?"

Ella just hugged her hard then gathered up the strips in one hand and the boxes in the other. "I'm throwing the boxes in the kitchen trash bag and tossing it in the garbage cans. Levi would have heart failure if he came home and saw them. Here, you hold on to these." She pushed the indicators into Missy's hands. "Then, we'll have some tea and discuss options. But you should know, whatever you decide, whatever you want or need, Levi and I will back you one hundred percent."

Two cups of tea and a stack of slightly charred toast later and they were done talking and ready to start doing. Missy had called her gynecologist in Naples and had miraculously snagged a late afternoon appointment. She accepted Ella's offer to go with her, though her initial reaction was to do it alone. They decided to go out for dinner afterward at their favorite Thai restaurant in Naples. It was perfect timing since Levi and probably Don would be playing poker that night at the Twisted Pelican.

Missy got up from the kitchen island and started to gather the dishes. "I'm just going to do my regular stuff today until it's time to leave for Naples. And you should, too, Ella. I know you've got writing to do today. I'll get the office supplies I bought yesterday out of the Volvo, then I'm going to bake." When Ella started to protest, Missy stopped her. "I have to keep busy today. Or I'm just going to curl up into a ball."

Later, much later, Missy climbed into bed, nudging Lady Marmalade out of its center, then pulling the cat into her arms. It had been a long, exhausting day. There had been sweet and funny texts from Don, who had spent the day immersed in framing and preliminary sketches for Levi's mural. His last message had come just moments ago. *"Poker game done. I'm $50 richer! Do you feel like company or is it too late? I want you. Ti amo. XO"*

She had texted back. *"The rich get richer. I'm curled up with Lady, almost asleep. I want you, too, but am too tired to do anything about it. Rain check? I love you too. XO"*

The visit to the gynecologist had confirmed what she already knew. She was pregnant—about nine weeks. Dinner and one small glass of wine—her last—with Ella confirmed what she had been feeling all day. She wanted the baby, she would keep the baby. Ella had happily agreed with her decision but had disagreed about when to tell Don. Ella argued for right away but Missy had not yet made up her mind about when and how she would break the news to him.

"Honey, I'm not arguing with you. But you already have a little tummy action going on and now that I know, I can see your boobs are definitely larger. Don's an artist, he's going to notice and it's going to be pretty soon."

"He paints landscapes and tractors, Ella. It's not like he specializes in nudes. But, yes, I agree. Don's going to notice and I don't want him to find out like that. I just need a few days to get used to the idea myself."

Missy drifted off to sleep with the images of pregnancy tests dancing through her dreams. It was not a restful night.

CHAPTER ELEVEN

How does a middle-aged man go from being satisfied and more than a little grateful that he has a sexy, funny, independent woman in his life with whom he can have uncomplicated sex a couple of times a week to a raging horn dog, mooning around like a high school boy with a crush on a pretty teacher? It was a million-dollar question for which Don had no answers. He was the man who had shaken his head with condescending amusement as he watched one after another of his friends and acquaintances on Mimosa Key—like Law Monroe and Mark Solomon—fall headlong into love. Many of the men were way older and much wiser than he. Look at Levi and Fitz!

The demands of matting and framing all the remaining paintings needed for Casa Blanca Resort and Spa and the prep work for the addition to Levi's mural commissioned by Ella had occupied most of his days. And making sweet love to Missy had consumed two of the nights. But Don found himself wanting her all the time. He'd even begun doodling little sketches of her, mostly pictures of her in the bathtub the night they had made their whispered proclamations of love.

Now, here it was Saturday night and instead of taking his lady love out on a date or, better yet, hunkering down with her in his big comfortable bed, he was standing in a freezing operating room, with cans of paint and a pile of tarp. Ella had dropped off the key Levi had made for him when he started this project over three years ago. Two walls were almost covered with Levi's toys, the last one of an orange ATV painted that summer. Don was going to fill in the remainder of the far wall with the painting of Ella and Hersch in the red Mustang. It would fit nicely and continue along on the white seashell drive that meandered through most of the mural on that wall.

The hours flew by as Don sketched in the drawing and started filling in background colors. The work was fun and lighthearted, done in acrylics in an almost comic book style. Not his usual medium these days, or the one that had brought him fame long ago in Italy, but he had fun with it. When he painted in Levi's surgery, he did not listen to opera as he did in his studio; instead, he played Levi's soundtrack of Jimmy Buffett.

Don stepped back from the painting to get a different perspective and let out a shout of surprise as he bumped into something. Not the cool hard surface of Levi's operating table, but the warm softness of his lover. He turned to find Missy doubled over in laughter, her long dark hair hiding her pretty face. After catching his breath from the shock of seeing another person in what he thought was a totally empty building, he walked over to the far wall, and switched off the sound system.

"You just took five years off my life! What are you doing here? How did you get in?"

Missy stood up and shook the keys in her hand. "Ella gave me her key when I told her I was worried that you hadn't eaten this evening. I brought you some mushroom barley soup I made today. Levi loves it for Hanukkah. Along with piles of potato latkes. But I'm not making those until Tuesday. I did bring some nice rolls, though, and some chocolate chip cookies. Are you hungry? Can you stop to eat?"

He was wiping his hands on a paint-stained cloth he tucked back into his jeans. "I'm starving." He pulled her into his arms. "For you." And then his lips crashed down on hers. Eventually, she pushed him away. "Stop. We can't do this here. You need to eat and then paint. Ella will kill me for interrupting you if it means this painting is not ready for her big reveal on Tuesday."

She stepped around him to inspect his progress while he dived into the bag of goodies.

"It looks amazing. You've done a great job with the background. You even have Levi's crazy crooked palm tree. And the red you are painting the Mustang is exactly right. I can't wait to see it when it is completed. Can I come again tomorrow to get a look at the final painting?"

"Yes, but I'm starting early tomorrow. I want to be finished by mid-day. No one is using this room until Wednesday when Levi has surgeries scheduled but it needs time to dry and then the room has to be cleaned and sterilized top to bottom. You could come by around noon if you like. But only if you bring more of these." Don had finished a cup of soup and half a roll and was already unwrapping the stack of still-warm chocolate chip cookies.

Missy laughingly agreed—she never baked less than four dozen cookies at a time. She continued to stare at the mural. "You know, I never noticed, but you haven't signed this mural. Are you waiting until you've painted the entire operating room?" When he didn't answer, she turned back to him.

Don was standing still, a partially eaten cookie halfway to his mouth. He hated signing his work with a fake name. Don Smith. It had fit his new persona but he was never really comfortable with the name. His signature on his paintings done in Florida was a messy scrawl with a prominent *D* and *S* and nothing else that was legible. He put the cookie down and walked over to Missy. It was time to peel away one more layer of secrecy for her. He loved her and he wanted her to love who he really was. He took her hands in his, he didn't want her to pull away from him when he finally spoke the truth.

"I hate signing paintings with the name Don Smith. That's not my real name. I'm Donatello Stampone." It was such a pleasure to say his name aloud. He searched her face for shock or anger. Instead, he saw a flicker of recognition in her eyes before her lips curved up into a broad grin. She was laughing at him.

"Well, it's really nice to meet you, Donatello. I love your name, it fits you. Don was much too ordinary a name for you. But it fit with Missy. An ordinary name for a quiet and ordinary woman."

He started to protest, shocked that she would describe herself as ordinary.

She cut him off with a giggle. "But, surprise, surprise. That's not my real name, either. I Anglicized it when I ran away from DC. I'm not Missy Edmond, my name is Melisande Emond." She made a little curtsey to him, her eyes searching his face.

He pulled her up and into his arms. "Melisande. It suits you. Beautiful just like you." He kissed her. This vibrant woman who had brought him back to life. "I'm finished for tonight. Come home with me, Melisande and let me make love to you like it is our first time. Like we have no secrets." His voice stumbled on those last words. He still kept one last secret from her—one he could not bring himself to tell her. Not yet.

Missy looked up at him with tears in her eyes. "Yes," she whispered, almost sadly. "Like we have no secrets."

The next morning found Don easing himself from his bed, being careful not to wake Missy. Melisande. He would always think of her by that name now. He had murmured it to her over and over again last night as they made sweet, slow, passionate love. Even with a few hours of sleep, he felt energized and eager to complete the mural. He hoped when he was done that he could take Missy away for a few days, someplace quiet and private, where he would tell her about Gina and Raphael.

Back in Levi's surgery, music blasting, Don went quickly to work on the remainder of the painting. Ella had given him several photographs from which he had drawn a composite. Sketched on the wall was Ella, only the back of her head visible, her hand waving goodbye to Levi. He mixed some paint to achieve the proper flesh tone for her arm and hand. His fingers shook as he blended the colors; it had been years since he had used these particular hues. Since he'd last painted Gina and Raphael. His boy would be fifteen now. What would he be like? Blonde, like Gina, but with his brown eyes. He'd seemed to have his height, but at three who could tell how tall he would have been as a young man?

Don shook his head to erase the memories. It was still too painful to remember the past. But, as he approached the mural, he realized he was trembling. He took a breath to steady himself, then began stroking color on the wall. It was all wrong. He wiped the paint away and began again. *No.* He stood staring without seeing what he had drawn, what he had begun. Instead he envisioned Ella's laughing face, full of love and full of hope. That's the gift he wanted to give his friends. Something cold and hard broke inside him as he began layering on the paint, creating a portrait of Ella, looking back over her shoulder, smiling at Levi as she waved good-bye.

Tears blurred his sight but he pushed on. Sunlight glinted off Ella's pale blond hair, not golden like Gina's, but almost silver. He finished with Hersch, his red tongue lolling out of the side of his mouth, amused at the crazy antics of his humans. Don stood before the painting, silent sobs shaking him, his arms hanging at his sides, the paintbrush still in his hand.

He felt gentle fingers take the brush from him, then soft but strong arms wrapped around him from behind. Missy's head pressed against his back as she held him, murmuring unintelligible but comforting words. Words that loosened the hold of the past, the painful memories of his loss.

"I never paint portraits anymore. I haven't painted a portrait in years." His voice was soft, tear-laden. "Not since my family died. Not since I lost my wife and my son."

Missy fell silent. He needed to see her. Don turned in the arms that still held him. And looked at the woman he loved. Her face was pale. Tears turned her blue eyes into a bottomless sea of hurt and confusion. He framed her face with his hands.

"I was married. My wife's name was Gina. We met in art school and that was it for me. She was wonderful, a talented artist in her own right, but her real passion was our family. We had a son, a golden child, who we named Raphael. They died twelve years ago, when he was three. A stupid car accident, on a twisty mountain road she'd driven a thousand times. No one's fault. It just happened. My life ended. I buried them and walked away. From our home, from Italy, from my career. I wandered for several years until I found this island and I made it my new home. But I still hung on to the past. I wouldn't paint portraits. I wouldn't be happy. I would never love again."

The tears spilled from her eyes. His rough thumbs brushed them away before he continued. "Then, I met you. And I was happy, but still I would not let go of the past. But, as I stood here, refusing to paint the face of the woman my best friend loves, refusing to allow her to give him a present from her heart, I knew I had to let the past go. I want to paint your beautiful face, the face that I love more than I ever thought I could love again."

Missy reached up to brush the tears from his cheeks. He bent his head to hers, but paused, waiting for permission, waiting for her to accept him, with all his secrets laid bare. She kissed him. His arms went around her and pulled her close, like a man clinging to a life preserver in a stormy sea. She melted into him and he poured all his love into the kiss.

She pulled away from him. Her eyes were clear, no more tears. Don brushed a finger over her lips that were swollen and reddened from their endless kiss. "*Ti amo, cara.* I love you. No more secrets. Can you love me, still? Now that you know everything about me?"

"I love you, Donatello. I love you—your past, the present, and our future. Can you love me, with all my secrets?" Her eyes searched his face.

"Melisande, I love you, yes. Secrets and all. But, really, what haven't you told me? A guilty pleasure? A secret crush from high school? An embarrassing middle name? I don't care. I love you." He bent to kiss her again, but she took a step back. She seemed nervous but excited, too.

"I have one more secret to share with you. I haven't kept it from you for long—I've only known a few days myself. It's more of a surprise, really. I had thought to make it my Christmas gift to you, then I thought maybe a Hanukkah present from me to you, since that is only two days away. But, it's as much your gift to me as it is my gift to you." She laughed, her throaty, sexy laugh. "Oh, I'm really making a total mess out of this, aren't I? I'm just going to tell you."

She took a deep breath. Her eyes were shining, full of love and hope. "We're going to have a baby."

At first, he thought he had not heard her correctly. Then for an instant he thought she had found the seascape he'd painted for her and had it matted and framed for him. But that made no sense. His mind was trying to work out the details of that but screeched to a halt when he heard her say "baby."

"Baby?" He almost squeaked the word.

"Yes, a baby. I'm about ten weeks pregnant. With your—our—baby." She was starting to crumble, her eyes still searching his face.

Joy like he had never believed he would feel again flooded through him. He dropped to his knees, reaching out for her, pulling her to him. Don buried his face against her rounded tummy, planting kisses as he thanked God for all the blessings of his life, in broken Italian and English. Missy must have gotten the message, because her arms encircled his shoulders and she rested her cheek on his bowed head.

"No more secrets, Donatello, just a lifetime of love and family and beauty."

"And maybe a few surprises, *cara*, just a few."

CHAPTER TWELVE

issy emerged from her bathroom, braiding her still damp hair. "I'm exhausted and my feet are killing me—whatever made me wear four-inch heels?" She glanced over at the blue Jimmy Choos Don had given her for Hanukkah. "I won't be wearing them for a while. But I'm glad I was dressed up for tonight—wasn't that such a fun time?"

Don looked up from where Lady Marmalade lay across his lap, purring as she demanded more petting, looking regal in her new rhinestone collar. He smiled an amused smile, his dark eyes reflecting the glow of the candles on her dresser she had lit earlier.

He looked good in her bed, her cat sprawled on his legs, his long talented fingers moving teasingly through the orange and white fluff, the cat's fur and Don's silver hair a pleasing contrast to the indigo comforter. "I'm still revved up from the dancing. Where did Lacey and Clay find that band? They were amazing! Or maybe it's the caffeine from the espresso and that chocolate Yule Roll? That was delicious!"

Missy stuck her tongue out at her lover. They had spent their first Christmas Eve together with all their friends at a party at Clay and

Lacey's house at Casa Blanca Resort and Spa. And it was also the first time they had appeared anywhere in Mimosa Key as a couple, a couple in love, holding hands and sneaking kisses. "I wouldn't know about the espresso or the Yule Roll since I had lemon ginger tea and fruitcake. No caffeine for me and the baby. I'm almost getting used to that, but I would still kill for a large coffee first thing in the morning!" Missy climbed into bed with her cat and her man. She reached a hand up to touch the driftwood frame of the dramatic seascape that hung above her white wicker headboard. "Clay cornered me and offered me almost anything I could name if I would let him have this painting. He almost cried when I told him 'no'."

Don tilted his head to look up and behind him at the depiction of sunrise he had painted for Missy only a few weeks ago and laughed. "I know. Levi made me almost the same offer. I told him I'd do some sunrises and sunsets from the beach here to make it up to him. I made the same offer to Clay." Before she could say anything, he cut her off. "I know. I told them it would be after the first of the year because my lady and I are treating ourselves to a sunny vacation in The Grenadines. Clay offered me an advance on the paintings. Maybe we should let people know we have plenty of money so they'll stop worrying about us."

Missy shook her head. "Let's keep our secrets a little longer. No one has to know that I booked that vacation as your Hanukkah/Christmas present from me. They can think all I gave you was the sexy shirt and nice pants you were wearing tonight and that we're sharing the cost for our trip to St. Vincent. We can let our friends know about our pasts—some of it, anyway—after we tell them about the baby. We'll do that when we return. We can't wait much longer than that because now Levi knows and he can't keep a secret." They'd told the good doctor the morning after Ella showed him the newest addition to his mural. He had been so excited that he'd given Missy the deed to the cottage and access to the Gulf as her Hanukkah present, with a promise to oversee any expansion of the cottage she might need in the future, with a wink to Don.

Don reached over and patted her round tummy. "Yeah, I agree. This little guy is getting bigger every day. I'm surprised your Yoga buddies haven't noticed. We need to let people in on our news pretty soon or they're just going to think you're getting fat." He chuckled at the image.

"I'm not getting fat. I'm the perfect weight for my stage of pregnancy. But, speaking of the little *guy*, I saw my OB-GYN yesterday while you were in Miami. She suggested I give you this for Christmas." Missy reached into her nightstand drawer and pulled out a square box, wrapped in red and green. "Merry Christmas!"

Don sent her a quizzical look as she handed him the gift. He ripped off the bow, much to Lady's delight as she immediately began batting it around the bed. Then she was playing in the strips of wrapping paper he'd torn off, completely oblivious to the stunned look on his face as he took the lid off the box. In a small shadow box frame, lined in pink satin, Missy had mounted the pregnancy test indicator that announced "pregnant" beneath the ultrasound photograph she had received the day before. Curling across the picture was a pink ribbon, with gold writing. "It's a Girl!"

"I love it. I love you! I love our baby girl!" Don was grinning, tears gathered in his beautiful brown eyes. "How did you manage this?" he asked, holding the frame out to her.

"I told you, I can Google how to do anything. Actually, I looked on Pinterest to see how people had announced the sex of their babies and I saw this so I tweaked it a little to make it ours." Her eyes searched his face. "Do you like it? I mean, are you okay that we're having a girl?"

"I am *so* okay with a little girl. I am over the moon. I love her already—almost as much as I love you!"

Don put his hand under her pillow to pull out a small velvet box, which he thrust into her now shaking hands. "This is what I was doing in Miami yesterday. Merry Christmas!"

Missy managed to unwrap the gift, with trembling fingers and her eyes blurred with tears. Inside was a stunning sapphire and diamond ring, very like Princess Diana's, but emerald-cut. Don pulled the ring out of its satin setting and slipped it on her finger. "Melisande, this isn't just a Christmas/Hanukkah present. This is an engagement ring. It will show the whole world how much I love you. Will you marry me?"

She looked down at the beautiful blue ring, shimmering in the candlelight, like the ultramarine sea outside her cottage shimmered with the dancing light from the southern stars. Then, she looked into the warm caring eyes of the man she loved, without reservation, without any secrets.

"Yes. I'll marry you. And I'll love you forever."

THE END

FROM MORGAN MALONE

Dear Readers,

I've loved reading romance since I was twelve and my dream was always to write love stories. I'm a lucky woman to be living my dream. *Color My World* is my fifth romance and my third novella set in Barefoot Bay. I was so excited to try my hand at a holiday story and I welcomed the opportunity to give Missy, Levi's housekeeper (and so much more) from *Shoulder to Lean On*, her own story. As is often the case, Missy and Don took the story in a direction I did not expect! But, I loved writing about their sorrowful pasts and the miracle of the holiday season that opened their hearts to love and trust. And I really enjoyed using some of my own experiences as a painter as I wrote about Don's creative process, though I work exclusively in watercolor.

I am so thrilled to be part of Rocki's Barefoot Bay World! I've found the perfect home there for my seasoned heroes and heroines: men and women, 40 and older, who are looking for a second chance romance or to fall in love for the last time in their lives. My next Barefoot Bay book is coming in 2019. The doctors of FL-Ortho are back with a Billionaire story, featuring Dr. Joel Alfonso. Too smart, too sexy and too elusive for all but one woman, lost to him for ten years, he must confront the love of his youth and risk everything to win her back.

I live near Saratoga Springs, NY, with my chocolate Labrador retriever, Marley. My children and my amazing grandson live nearby.

I'd love to hear from you. Please visit me

On Facebook: https://www.facebook.com/morgan.malone39,

on Twitter: @MMaloneAuthor,

or at my website: http://www.morganmaloneauthor.com.

If you enjoyed *Color My World*, please consider telling others and writing a review on one of the online booksellers or Goodreads.

Thank you and I hope this story gives brings you all the joy and wonder of the holidays!

Morgan

ALSO AVAILALE BY MORGAN MALONE

Cocktales: An After-50 Dating Memoir
Unanswered Prayers

Love In Control Series

Out of Control: Kat's Story
Taking Control: Rick's Story

Barefoot Bay Series

Shoulder to Lean On: a Barefoot Bay World novella
Need You Now: a Barefoot Bay World novella

Made in the USA
Monee, IL
29 May 2023

34408125R00056